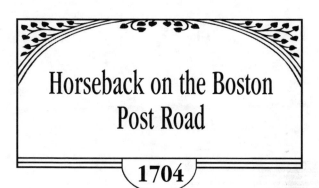

Horseback on the Boston Post Road

1704

Books by Laurie Lawlor

The Worm Club
How to Survive Third Grade
Addie Across the Prairie
Addie's Long Summer
Addie's Dakota Winter
George on His Own
Gold in the Hills
Little Women *(a movie novelization)*

Heartland series
Heartland: Come Away with Me
Heartland: Take to the Sky
Heartland: Luck Follows Me

American Sisters series
West Along the Wagon Road 1852
A *Titanic* Journey Across the Sea 1912
Voyage to a Free Land 1630
Adventure on the Wilderness Road 1775
Crossing the Colorado Rockies 1864
Down the Río Grande 1829
Horseback on the Boston Post Road 1704

American
SISTERS
Horseback on the Boston Post Road
1704

Laurie Lawlor

A MINSTREL® HARDCOVER
PUBLISHED BY POCKET BOOKS

New York   London   Toronto   Sydney   Singapore

A MINSTREL HARDCOVER

 A Minstrel Book published by
POCKET BOOKS, a division of Simon & Schuster, Inc.
1230 Avenue of the Americas, New York, NY 10020

ISBN: 0-671-03923-7

First Minstrel Books hardcover printing December 2000

10   9   8   7   6   5   4   3   2   1

Cover illustration by Dennis Lyall

Printed in the U.S.A.

For Rebecca Burton Mills,
who helped take care of
Sis and Sis

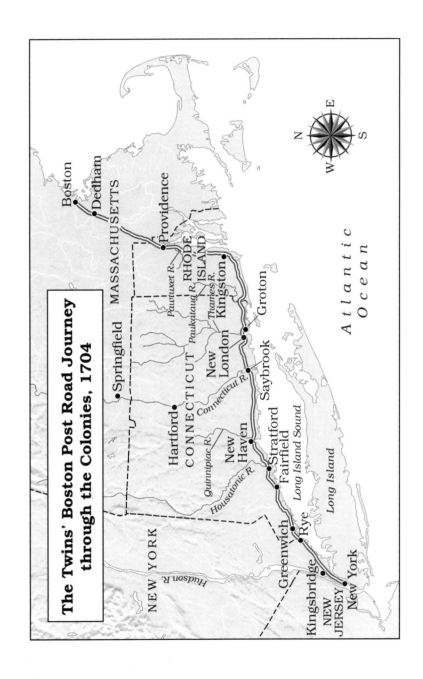

The Twins' Boston Post Road Journey through the Colonies, 1704

Boston
Dedham
Providence
MASSACHUSETTS
Pawtuxet R.
RHODE ISLAND
Paukataug R.
Thames R.
Kingston
Groton
Springfield
New London
CONNECTICUT
Connecticut R.
Saybrook
Hartford
New Haven
Stratford
Fairfield
Quinnipiac R.
Housatonic R.
Long Island Sound
Long Island
NEW YORK
Greenwich
Rye
Hudson R.
Kingsbridge
NEW JERSEY
New York
Atlantic Ocean

N
E
W
S

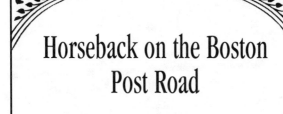

Horseback on the Boston Post Road

1704

Introduction

The first mail in North America was sent from New York City on January 22, 1673, and arrived in Boston on about February 5th. Nobody knows the name of the first postrider, but everyone knows the route he took through New Haven, Springfield, Brookfield, Worcester, and Cambridge. The route was later called the Boston Post Road — the first link in what would one day become a 3,000-mile chain of trails and roads that would span the continent from the Atlantic to the Pacific Oceans.

A little more than two decades after the first postrider made his trip, another important and unusual person followed the same route. Her name was Sarah Kemble Knight. She was a thirty-eight-year-old Boston shopkeeper who was keen-eyed and sharp-tongued, and, fortunately for posterity, she kept a diary about her 270-mile journey on horseback. It was an unusual trip at the time for a woman to make independently. She faced swollen rivers without bridges, plus bears, winter storms, uncertain accommodations, bad food, and, often, bad directions. On occasion she took advantage of the company and presence of postriders, who carried the mail for colonists.

This novel is based on her wonderful diary, which was published for the first time in 1825. Only a few facts are known for certain about Sarah Knight. She was born on April 19, 1666, had one daughter, and spent most of her life in Boston. She was widowed at an early age. A unique and independent woman for her time, she managed to develop keen business skills and knowledge of the law. She ran a shop and a farm, operated an inn, and purchased and sold several hundred acres of land. She died September 25, 1727, was buried in New London, Connecticut, and left behind for her daughter the sizable sum of 1,800 pounds.

Chapter 1

"We have no birthday."

"Doesn't matter."

"Who's older?"

"Not important."

Hester sighed. In eerie, matching movements she and her twelve-year-old twin sister, Philena, scrubbed the keeping-room floor of the house on Moon Street. *Dip-twist-slop-circle right-circle left.* Every week followed a familiar pattern. Monday— washing; Tuesday—ironing; Wednesday—mending; Thursday—churning; Friday—cleaning; Saturday— baking; Sunday—Sabbath. Days and weeks and months and years rolled in and out as predict- ably as the tides in Boston Harbor. Nothing ever seemed to change except the weather and the seasons.

Hester paused to watch Philena work. *I remember her dreams. She feels my pain. I used to find this reassuring. Now sometimes her face seems repulsive. May God forgive me.*

"What?" Philena said and frowned.

"Nothing," Hester replied quickly. She turned away so that her sister could not see her blush.

"Aren't you going to help? Can't do this all myself," Philena said. She sat back on her heels and dipped the rag in the bucket, then smacked the wet rag hard on the floor. *We are a pair of hands: she the right, and I the left. Exactly the same, except that she is always better.*

Hester smiled. Her sister should be more careful. It was so easy to read her thoughts—as easy as it was for Philena to read hers. On hands and knees, without looking at each other, the sisters danced their rags across nicks and knotholes that stared like eyes. Their rags *hush-hushed* across the broad pine boards and waltzed around the legs of the stools and the legs of the long plank table where the girls ate their meals with Madame Knight's boarders.

To keep her clothing clean as she worked, Hester had rolled up the waist of the black-and-white silk crepe petticoat and white shift, the cast-off clothes of Polly, Madame Knight's fifteen-year-old daughter. Philena did not care that her plain muslin apron was already soiled at the knees or that the hem of the front of her worn, dark-green shift was soggy.

Like her sister, Philena kept her long brown hair parted in the middle and tucked under a white cap that hid overlarge ears. Both girls had the same dark eyes and the same pale skin and the same thin lips. Except for their clothing, they were the same. Their voice, their laughter. The loping way they walked. The birdlike way they fluttered their hands when they were nervous. The careless way they chewed their food. Everything about them was identical. Even the secret name they had given each other was the same: Hester-Phina.

Since before they were born they had been together. As babies they slept curled in the same cradle, one sister sucking the other's thumb. They shared everything: trencher, spoon, mug, clothes, comb, blanket, bed. The only possessions they kept from each other were their thoughts. And even these sometimes escaped into communal use if they weren't careful.

Very, very careful.

Hester and Philena's lives had become so predictable, so alike, so inseparable that they could never have guessed how everything would suddenly change that bright October morning in 1704.

A little bell rang in the shop that adjoined the keeping-room. "Customer," Hester said. She tilted her head toward the open shop door. A gust of unseasonably warm wind from the busy Boston streets mingled with the shop's smells of ink powder, dried codfish, lead pencils, lamp black, chocolate, coffee, and linseed oil.

Footsteps. From where Hester and Philena crouched on the keeping-room floor, they had a fine view of customers' shoes and pant legs and skirt hems. Hester gave her sister the sign to begin the Game. They both knew the rules. One cough meant yes. Two meant no. The Game's only question never altered: *Is this one our mother?*

The customer's black shoes were scuffed and worn down so unevenly at the heels that she walked in a painful, lopsided manner. What they could see of her patched skirt was muddy and torn. Hester coughed twice loudly. This could not be the one. *Too poor, too pathetic.* In her mind, their mother was rich. She never walked anywhere. She rode in a carriage with two fine white horses. The fact that she had given Hester and Philena away as babies must have been a simple, youthful mistake. Perhaps she had never forgiven herself. Perhaps she longed to find them again.

Philena peered at the customer's battered shoes and coughed once. She felt hopeful. She always felt hopeful that they would be reunited. And yet she was realistic. A poor woman could not afford to keep twins who were hungry and bawling all the time. It made sense that their mother had been an unfortunate soul, a hapless victim of poverty.

Neither Hester nor Philena ever thought much about their father. They lived in a household ruled by women. Polly had a mother. Madame Knight had a mother. Goodwife Kemble had a mother — long dead but still discussed with so much vehemence that she seemed alive and quarrelsome as ever. To have a proper mother was a measure of one's worth. To not know who their real mother was always made Hester and Philena feel disconnected and disembodied, like smoke or mist. They had no birth story, no early, warm mother-memory—nothing to hold on to but each other.

"Thou art Madame Sarah Knight?" the customer asked in a tired, thin voice. She addressed their mistress in the formal, respectful way that was the custom between strangers.

"I am," Madame Knight answered impatiently from behind the counter.

There was a short pause, and then as quickly as the scuffed shoes had appeared, they shuffled across the floor. The bell rang. The door shut. The customer vanished.

"Wrong again," Hester hissed. She wrung out the rag. "If she were the one, she'd have asked for us."

"Maybe she doesn't know we're here," Philena said softly and pushed up her damp sleeves. "It was eleven years ago. A long time."

Hester snorted. She liked her grand story better. The carriage and the fine white horses. If she were going to be rescued from the life of an indentured maidservant, she wanted a marvelous improvement. "What use is there in trading one life of hardship for another?"

Philena didn't answer. Instead she began scrubbing again, harder and fiercer than before. *She always has to have the last word.*

Hester decided to cheer her sister, who took the Game much too seriously. She sang:

"Oh, Cape Cod girls they have no combs,
Heave away, heave away!
They comb their hair with codfish bones.
Heave away, heave away!
Heave away, you bully, bully boys!
Heave away, and don't you make a noise,
For we're bound for Australia!"

Philena joined her sister in a crooning duet:

"Oh, Cape Cod boys they have no sleds.
They slide down hill on codfish heads.
Heave away, heave away!"

Philena giggled, glad not to feel angry anymore. She could never stay mad at Hester very long.

"Oh, Cape Cod cats they have no tails,
They blew away in heavy—"

"Enough of that disreputable song!" Madame Knight shouted from the shop doorway, one pudgy fist on her wide hip. In her other fist she held a crumpled piece of paper. Her face was flushed and her blue eyes blazed. She was a short, stout woman of middle age with a famous temper that once again seemed about to explode.

Hester and Philena exchanged looks of caution. *Now what's wrong?*

"Why my old mother taught that horrid song to you, I shall never understand," Madame Knight declared.

"But Mistress—" Philena protested.

"Goodwife Kemble told us it is a proper working song," Hester added. She considered it her duty to finish her sister's sentences for her, especially when she knew that what Philena intended to say was not going to sound particularly convincing.

"It's a working song for sailors," Madame Knight said with great vehemence. She jammed a lock of graying hair into her second-best lace cap. "Let me remind you that *you* are not sailors. You are maidservants. This is not a ship and my mother must one day realize that. Oh, woe is me to be a poor widow in such an impossible situation! Perfidious servants who can't be trusted, a mother who thinks she's still on her father's sloop, and a daughter with impossible, grand fancies."

Hester shot an amused glance at her sister. *Polly's impossible, that's true enough.* Philena bit her lip and tried not to grin.

"Perhaps," Madame Knight growled, "I should forbid you to spend so much time with my mother. She is not a proper influence."

"We love and respect Goodwife Kemble," Hester said and made a fawning little curtsy. Every word she said was true. No one was quite as dear to them as Goodwife Kemble. Although the elderly woman had a habit of wandering off course sometimes and forgetting where she was, she told the most exciting stories about pirates who cruised the coast. And she was the one person in the Moon Street household who ever showed them the least bit of affection.

Madame Knight took a deep breath and glanced about the keeping-room. "How much pewter have we left?"

"A few plates. A bowl," Hester said. She knew exactly what was in the wooden cupboard against the wall. It was her job to polish the pieces that had not already been traded for cash. "Why do you ask, Mistress?"

Madame Knight did not answer. When her gaze fell on the only chair in the room, the one with the faded embroidered pillow, she scowled. "God rest his soul," she mumbled bitterly. She seemed to be speaking directly to her late husband, whose untimely death had caused her sudden fall in fortune. Madame Knight turned to the girls again. "I have much to do and I do not know how I'll manage before this afternoon. What time is it?"

Hester and Philena shrugged. Mentioning the missing clock at this particular moment did not seem like a very safe idea. Had Madame Knight already forgotten she had traded the clock to pay for last year's firewood?

"It's late and this may be my last chance. My very last chance. I will speak with you when I return. A matter of great urgency has come up," Madame Knight said. She hurriedly stuffed the paper into her pocket, which hung from a string tied around her ample middle.

Hester cleared her throat. "I can go to market for you," she volunteered. She liked nothing better than to put a basket on her arm and wander aimlessly among the colorful stalls of fish and vegetable vendors near the noisy harbor.

Madame Knight shook her head in a distracted fashion as she picked out a few plates from the cupboard and wrapped them in her apron. "This will be a much longer journey than a mere trip to market," she said. "Watch the shop for me. I will be back in a trice." She hurried out on to Moon Street.

"What was that all about?" Philena asked.

"A longer journey," Hester said. She quickly finished the floor and stood up. "Nothing that concerns us, I'm sure. We never go anywhere."

"But she said it did. She said she wishes to speak with us. 'A matter of great urgency.' That must mean something bad."

"Why do you always worry so much? Certainly she has more chores for us. Nothing else."

Philena pouted. "I do not like the sound of it."

"Be still," Hester replied. "And help me dump this bucket."

Together they lifted the heavy bucket by the handle and staggered outside. For several moments they stood in the small grassy spot behind the house, out of the wind. The sun warmed the tops of their heads and their shoulders. And for several moments, they luxuriated in doing nothing.

"Pssst!" Cato called. He peeked around the corner of the house. "Madame gone?"

"Yes," Philena replied, glad to see him. But before Philena could ask him how he was and where he had been, Hester interrupted.

"She'll be back soon," Hester warned. "Hurry now. What news?"

Cato leaned against the weatherbeaten house with the exaggerated laziness of the old men who gathered on the village green. "Much news maybe," Cato said and smiled at Hester as if Philena were not there.

Philena sighed. Shyly, she studied Cato's broad tawny face and laughing black eyes. Her only friends already belonged to her sister. Cato was Hester's friend. He worked outdoors and did the heavy work. He unloaded the merchandise and took care of Madame Knight's four horses. Barely fourteen, he had been a slave since he was taken as a very young boy from his Indian family in the Carolinas. Unlike Hester and Philena, he would receive no Freedom Dues when his time was up. He would always be a slave. That was just the way things were, Hester always reminded Philena. Some people were free. Some people were indentured servants who had to work a certain amount of time for their masters without pay. And some people were slaves. The same way that some people had mothers and some people didn't.

"Speak, boy!" Hester urged. She looked to her left and right. Any moment Madame Knight might come bustling up the narrow street and end their conversation and free time.

"I hear Madame say she make money soon. Lots of money," Cato said slyly. "She say she be rich."

"Where did you hear that?" Hester demanded.

"She come out the shop. Right away she a-calling to Master Thatcher across the way. She a-smiling and a-waving. Very bright and happy. So happy, she not kick me when I pass." Then he added in a low, confidential voice, "Even so, I going fast out of here."

Hester rolled her eyes. Cato was always bragging about running away, even though they all knew the punishment if he were caught. A severe beating and maybe the loss of one ear. And yet he said he didn't care. He said he was determined to escape back to his tribe in the wilderness of the Carolinas. No one would dare follow him.

"Madame Knight won't get rich selling a few more pewter plates," Philena scoffed. "She must have some new scheme."

"Maybe she know where pirate treasure," Cato suggested. His dark eyes glimmered. "Captain Kidd bury Spanish gold on hidden beach before they hang him. Maybe she go dig and get rich."

Philena licked her lips. The famous English pirate, Captain Kidd, had been captured and hung three years earlier. His short, violent life was told to them with great eagerness by Goodwife Kemble, who read of his exploits in broadsheets and newspapers that came all the way from London. These well-worn pages circulated up and down Moon Street. "They say he hid jewels and doubloons and pieces of eight in a sea chest. Madame Knight might —"

"Might what? If you believe everything Cato says," Hester interrupted with a nasty laugh, "you are a bigger fool than I thought."

Cato frowned. Philena felt herself shrinking.

Once again she became the left hand. The one of lesser rank. The one bitterly rebuked for not being clever, for being awkward and wanting a graceful manner.

"How you know Captain Kidd not make her rich?" Cato declared angrily. "She find treasure and you be sorry."

"Ahoy!" a shrill voice called from the kitchen window.

"Goodwife Kemble," Hester and Philena murmured. Instantly, Cato vanished.

Chapter

2

"Drop anchor and come aboard, Girl," Goodwife Kemble demanded. She swung open the shutter for a better view. Long ago she had given up calling either twin anything but Girl.

Hester sighed. Philena fidgeted. "We're busy, Mistress," Hester called back to her. Hester knew if they went inside to talk to Goodwife Kemble, they'd be trapped in the kitchen for hours.

"Not too busy to make fast," Goodwife Kemble replied, her raspy voice rising. She had good strong pipes when she gave orders. "I haven't heard your catechism. Now splice your patience and cruise down along into the galley. Be quick."

Reluctantly, Hester left the bucket beside the

back-door step. She and her sister trudged into the house. The old woman kept the kitchen as neat and trim as the deck of a well-run ship. Although she was nearly fourscore years, Goodwife Kemble was spry enough to climb out on to the roof to repair shingles or scamper up a ladder to wash the second-floor windows. She said she liked to go aloft, and protested loudly when her daughter ordered her down.

"So, I hear you're going to sea," Goodwife Kemble said. She sat on a bench with a gray shawl wrapped around her thin shoulders. She held the worn head of her cane in her gnarled hands.

Hester shrugged. "Madame Knight said something about a journey. She didn't mention anything about taking us along."

"She's not taking both of you. Just one. You." Goodwife Kemble lifted the tip of her cane and gave Hester a nudge. "That's why I want to hear your catechism. You set sail today."

"Today?" Hester said in amazement.

"Where?" Philena bleated. "Why?"

"My daughter won't say," Goodwife Kemble confessed, then added in a hushed tone, "I warned her she's sailing too close to the wind. But there's no stopping her when she's in this reckless state of mind."

Hester winked at her sister. *Just another of her fancies. Pay her no mind.* "Now, now, Mistress . . ." she began, half-smiling.

"Don't 'mistress' me. I've sounded it out. She's going. And she's taking one of you and Polly with her. Now say your catechism, the both of you," Goodwife Kemble commanded.

Only one of us? Philena gulped. To humor the ancient woman, she and Hester did as they were told.

"Come now and stand still beside each other," Goodwife Kemble said when they were finished.

"Do we have to?" Miserably, Philena twisted her apron. "Madame Knight says—"

"We must watch the shop while she's away," Hester interrupted.

Goodwife Kemble frowned. She had lost most of her teeth. When she scowled, her pitifully tooth-shaken mouth seemed to collapse like bread dough. It was difficult for Hester or Philena to believe that she had once been the most beautiful woman to ever sail 'round the Horn.

"My Sarah's too fat and too old to be wandering

the countryside rigged on a horse," Goodwife Kemble said. "What if she meets with Indians or bears or wolves? She can't shoot a gun. And what if the weather turns owlish? What if there's a gale? What then? You remember last winter—a season of more than ordinary cold and wind and deep snow. Why must she go in October, with bad weather ahead? She says nothing, but acts sly and says I'll be taken care of handsomely when she returns. How can she think that delivering the personal belongings of Mr. Trowbridge to his family will afford her such a great reward?"

Hester and Philena exchanged secret glances. *Great reward?* They had always considered Mr. Trowbridge a miserly, lonely, crooked-backed man. He had been one of Madame Knight's many boarders. Before he died, he had worked as a scrivener—a job Goodwife Kemble explained to mean a person who worked in a lawyer's office writing on pieces of paper in beautiful penmanship. He passed away one evening two weeks before and had been quickly buried. All that he left behind were some clothing and a mysterious, small trunk that was locked tight. Perhaps Madame Knight was being promised something valuable in Mr. Trowbridge's will.

Philena winked at her sister. *Maybe gold coins hidden in the trunk. Just like Captain Kidd's sea chest.*

"Girl!" Goodwife Kemble leaned forward and examined closely each of the twelve-year-old maidservants. "You can't fool me. I raised you, don't forget. I know all your impudent tricks. Now hold still for once."

Reluctantly, Hester and Philena froze. With elbows intertwined they seemed like a set of pale, identical roots found beneath a rotting log or an apple split perfectly in half or the same line of a hymn sung over and over. It was dizzying to look upon them at the same time. The startled eye moved from one to the other and back again as if to ask, "Can this be? Which is which? Who is who?"

Once a week for as long as they could remember, Goodwife Kemble ordered them to say their catechism and then stand beside each other for her inspection. "Stand up straight," she barked. She reached out with her cane and pushed Hester closer to Philena. "Who is tallest?"

"She is," Philena said, not bothering to look up.

"Who is smartest?"

"She is," Philena said. She glanced at her grinning twin sister.

"Who is the prettiest?" Goodwife Kemble demanded.

"She is," Philena mumbled, even though they had been told all their lives that they looked exactly alike.

"Who is the most patient, prudent, and prayerful?"

"She is," Philena said.

"Who is the most dutiful, kind, and loving?"

For a long moment Philena paused. "She is," she said finally. She felt a choking inside her throat. *What if Hester really does leave me behind?*

"God go with you," Goodwife Kemble said and studied Philena closely. She bowed her head and made an extra silent prayer. "Amen."

"But you said I'm not the one who's leaving," Philena protested, her voice quavering.

Goodwife Kemble glared at Philena. "Do not be saucy and impudent with me, Girl! I know exactly *who* you are."

Philena whispered her apology and made a little curtsy. She felt glad when Hester grabbed her arm and pulled her outdoors. But just as they stumbled toward freedom, Madame Knight caught them both by the necks of their dresses and hauled them into the house again like two flounders dangling from a hook.

Before they could protest, they found themselves standing in the middle of the keeping-room. Goodwife Kemble hobbled in from the kitchen and took a seat in the corner. "Is it true?" Philena asked Madame Knight.

"Goodwife Kemble said—"

"A journey today—"

"But I won't go."

"Can you ever speak without interrupting each other?" Madame Knight demanded. She dabbed her sweating forehead with a handkerchief. "Your habits are most irritating."

"Sorry," Hester said.

"Sorry," Philena echoed.

"I wished to tell you myself," Madame Knight said. She paced before them. "Once again my mother has completely disregarded my instructions."

Goodwife Kemble beamed happily. She liked nothing better than a bit of mutiny now and then.

"We leave this afternoon," Madame Knight continued.

This afternoon. Hester and Philena's faces filled with shock. Their mouths hung open in disbelief. *Can it be possible?* The idea of separation stunned them. For several moments they could not think of anything to say. Philena stared at a knothole. Hester studied her dirty feet.

And then Hester began to weep. Of course when she began to weep, so did Philena. Soon they were both wailing louder and louder until Madame Knight put her hands over her ears and had to shut the front door for fear that the neighbors would think she was abusing her servants.

"Enough!" Madame Knight cried. "It is only a journey. We leave today and we shall return as soon as we can. There is not a moment to lose. We are already late in our departure. I need one of you to stay here to watch the shop and help my mother. I need one of you to go to assist me and Polly. What is more simple to understand than that?"

Neither Hester nor Philena was willing to understand. All that they knew was that their lives would be wrenched apart. The thought was as painful as if they were both about to have an arm torn away.

"I cannot go," Hester choked between sobs. "I cannot."

"Do not make her," Philena protested. "She is all that I have in the world."

"You thankless wights!" Madame Knight declared. "I took you in out of the goodness of my heart. I raised you. When the Boston authorities brought you to me, scrawny as a pair of stray cats, I said I'd feed you and dress you and house you. Bring you up as proper Christians. For what? A few miserable shillings a year they give me. You *owe* me your time. You owe me far more than just that. You owe me your lives."

Hester and Philena shivered as if the room had suddenly become very cold.

"You will do as I say," Madame Knight said, "or you will find yourselves in worse circumstances. Your time can be disposed of easily enough. I could send one of you to Virginia. Do not cross me on this." Her gray eyes looked hard. Her mouth's expression was stony.

Philena rubbed her face with her dirty sleeve. Hester sniffed loudly. They had heard this story and this threat countless times. They knew they still had nine years left on their indentured contract. In nine years they would reach their majority—age twenty-one—and they would be free. Until then, Madame Knight could split them apart anytime she wished and sell their remaining time to anyone who wanted to buy a servant's services. And the very worst place for a servant was Virginia. Some rumors said it was the hard labor and the beatings. Others claimed it was the heat and the disease. Whatever the reason, servants sent to Virginia plantations were never heard from again.

"Come now, Girl," Goodwife Kemble said gently to sniffling Hester and Philena. "You'll simply keep your weather eye peeled and you'll be reunited when spring comes again. That's not so far off. Why don't you both go above deck for some fresh air? You're going to make yourself pretty nigh fin out if you keep up your blubbering."

Gratefully, Hester and Philena stumbled out the back door. They walked down the path to the rail fence that separated Madame Knight's property from the common pasture. "We could run away," Philena suggested.

"You sound as foolish as Cato."

"You could pretend you were ill and unable to travel."

"She'd simply take you instead." Hester cocked her head. Beyond the pasture they heard the *clank-*

clank-clank of the blacksmith shoeing horses. *For the journey.*

Hester blew her nose loudly. "And I suppose you know why Madame Knight chose me for the journey?"

"Because you are the tallest, prettiest, smartest, most kind, dutiful, and loving?"

Hester made a face and shook her head. She felt surprised by how wretchedly stupid her sister could be sometimes. "She picked me to go with her to keep me out of trouble — far from home and far away from the shop. She left the good twin behind. I've heard her tell Goodwife Kemble that you're the pliable one. The one who never vexes or contradicts. The one who always counts correctly the customers' pence for the pins and needles and thread. She trusts you."

"You confess your faults too easily, Hester-Phina," Philena replied.

Hester smiled at the sound of their special name. It seemed a kind of comfort. She watched Philena sit on a stump and pick a scraggly sprig of wayward mint. Philena twirled it between her callused fingers. The sharp green smell reminded her of biting salt spray along the ocean when they went to gather clams. By the time Hester returned, it might be spring again. *Clamming season.* That was what Goodwife Kemble had said. Spring seemed like a long way away.

"Don't look so sad. Now you're making me miserable, too," Hester said and frowned. "What choice do we have? None. You know that. I must go. And soon I'll return and everything will be just the way it was before I left. I promise."

Philena slumped forward. "We have never been apart. Never." She crushed the mint in her fist, then tossed it as far as she could. "I think I might die without you."

Hester gave her a playful shove. "You will be fine. I will be fine, too," she said in a bright voice.

But they both knew she wasn't telling the truth.

"Girls, that's enough lying about lag-last, shiftless, and useless," Madame Knight bellowed from the doorway. She gathered her long skirt to keep it from the mud and hurried out of the house. Over one plump arm she carried a basket filled with gifts from their neighbors. Jams and jellies and fresh bread wrapped in clean cloth. "There is work to be done. And Polly? Where is she? We will never be ready to leave at this rate."

"Haven't seen her, Mistress," Hester replied. Madame Knight's only daughter was the apple of her eye. Polly could do no wrong. Over the years Hester and her sister had learned that it was safest not to speak when Polly's name was mentioned. Saying anything almost always landed them in trouble.

"Come here and take this," Madame Knight said. When the girls came closer, Philena took the basket from her. "Which one are you? Doesn't matter. See what you can fit into the tuck-a-muck. And don't forget the box of food when it's time to leave. We shall be lucky to find decent provisions not outrageously priced at inns along the Post Road."

While Philena disappeared into the kitchen, Hester followed Madame Knight to the barn. "Mistress, can you tell me where we're going?" Hester asked.

"No, I cannot," Madame Knight replied. "I have been told not to reveal our destination."

Mr. Trowbridge's relatives are certainly a suspicious lot! Hester decided to rethink her strategy. "What route shall we travel?" she asked innocently while inspecting the three enormous, restless horses.

They looked down at her with big eyes and stomped their big hooves. They curled their lips to reveal long, sharp, yellow teeth. The sight nearly took her breath away.

"We will ride south along the Post Road," Madame Knight said, "toward New York."

"We are going to New York?" Hester asked. She felt sick to her stomach. She had only ridden half a dozen times in her life. "Is that not very far?"

"I did not say we are going to New York, Girl. I said we are riding in that direction."

Suddenly, Hester felt confused and disheartened. *Doesn't she know exactly where she's going?* She looked into the eyes of her mistress's horse and did not feel the least bit of confidence. The villainously ugly creature of faded, sunburned sorrel color had a crazy, wild glare. The other two horses, called pacers, were so abnormally broad-backed and broad-bodied that riding them would be like sitting on a table with her feet hanging over the side, resting on the sidesaddle's double stirrups. She and Polly would practically need ladders to climb atop their backs. Even so, there was always the possibility of falling off or being knocked to the ground. *This journey is headed toward disaster.* "Mistress, why can you not—"

"You know the old saying," Madame Knight warned, " 'Curiosity killed the cat.' I suggest you ask no more questions—"

"Mama?" Polly cried. She scurried around the barn. The whites of her large gray eyes were red. Her pale face was streaked with tears. "I cannot go with so few dresses. It isn't fair. What will people think when they see me wearing the same dress over and over again? I will be humiliated."

Madame Knight took a deep breath. She put her dimpled fists on her broad hips and looked at her pretty, wailing daughter. "We have no choice, my dear. There is not space."

"I won't go then," Polly announced.

Hester breathed a great sigh of relief. She would be glad to make this ill-fated trip without the bothersome, spoiled creature.

"We have already discussed this," Madame Knight replied mysteriously. "This is your opportunity to meet quality people. You have never been outside of Boston. Now, my dear, please dry your eyes and finish packing your clothing. I am sure that we will find plenty of fine dressmakers in New Haven."

New Haven! Hester scowled. They were going all the way to New Haven for a new wardrobe for Polly?

Madame Knight's comment seemed to make perfect sense to her daughter. With revived spirits, Polly shoved her way past Hester. "Out of my way, Girl," she snarled and marched back to the house.

Hester could not retaliate. Not with Madame Knight watching. *Just wait,* she thought.

It was nearly three o'clock before the horses were saddled and Mr. Trowbridge's belongings were fastened with ropes behind Madame Knight's saddle. She and Polly and Hester said their final, tearful farewells before setting off behind fat Captain Luist, who promised to accompany them as far as the first town on the Post Road. A small group of neighbors and friends followed the horseback riders to the place where Moon Street forked. "Good-bye! Good-bye!" they shouted.

Philena stood outside the shop and waved a handkerchief and sobbed as if her heart would break. She could not believe that Hester was really leaving. All afternoon she had denied that such a thing would happen. As she watched her sister ride away, she felt a terrible wrenching emptiness that throbbed like a toothache. *What will I do without Hester?*

Hester took one look back at her sister standing in the muddy street. Hester blinked hard and tried to appear brave as the sidesaddle rocked dangerously from side to side. *Indians. Cold wind. Deep snow. Bears and wolves.*

As she moved farther and farther away from Philena, she felt as if she were watching herself becoming smaller and smaller. A memory returned. Hester recalled when she was a little girl and glanced for the first time into Madame Knight's looking glass. She thought she was seeing her sister smile and reach out to her. She even tried to lift and look behind the looking glass, certain that Hester-Phina must be hiding there. When she discovered her sister had vanished, Hester burst into tears and cried inconsolably.

That was how she felt at this very moment: abandoned and alone.

Chapter

3

On Friday afternoon I, Polly Knight, leave home in Company with my Deer Mother and our madeservant who is most disagreeable & tedious & complains mightily about her horse who is abnormally broadbacked & slow. I wish she did not join us. Weather clear. I keep this record of our Travel to remynd me that disappointments & Enjoyments are often so blended together, by the good Providence of God, that comfort may be drawn by the Prudent Man, even amidst tryals and difficulties. This being my first true Journey away from home I am eager to gaze upon Marvels in taverns such as a Fine Large White bear brought from Greenland or a Sapient Dog who can light lamps, Spell, read and Tell tyme. I Have heard *of such things from my Dear friend Mehitable Parkman who is better than any Sister. This Afternoon jolly Captain Luist travels with us as far as Dedham, where we plan to meet the Postrider heading West. Captain tells us Frightfull tales of Indians & Skalpings but Mother is determined to Procede even tho no postrider comes. We rest ourselves then go on Alone. 12 Miles to the place where we will spend the Night. What they call the Post Road is little more than a trampled Cow path between trees some places. God keep us Safe.*

—Polly Knight

Weary and sore, Madame Knight, Polly, and Hester arrived at an inn called the Good Woman Tavern that evening. A great painted sign hung over the door showing a figure of a woman with no head. "What is the meaning of that?" Polly demanded. "She has no face. We cannot see her eyes or her mouth. How do we know she is good?"

"Perhaps she is good because she is headless and therefore silent," Hester muttered. She had had nearly enough of Polly's incessant chatter about the color of the maples and were they nearly as bright as the ones back in Boston and how she would like to see the militia drill in New Haven and could they possibly be better dressed and more dignified than the ones back in Boston? Hester was glad when she could climb down from her horse, stretch her weary limbs, and escape from Polly's grating voice.

"I shall do the talking to the innkeeper," Madame Knight announced. It took Hester and Polly and a groomsman with a crooked leg to help lower her from her horse. She was wearing a sad-colored woolen round gown of camlet made with puffed sleeves that came to her pudgy elbows and were finished with knots of ribbons and ruffles. On her head she wore a close round cap that did not cover her ears. She adjusted her heavy woolen short cloak on her shoulders and carefully counted the three saddlebags and tuck-a-muck containing their food. She instructed the lame groomsman to carry these inside where they'd be safe, and woe to him if he dropped or damaged or lost anything. The horses were led to the barn to be unsaddled and fed.

With great dignity Madame Knight pulled open the heavy wooden door. The sight of her mistress's purple gloves of soft kid startled Hester. *Where did these come from?* The bright gloves extended to Madame Knight's elbows. Surely the minister at the meeting house back in Boston would never have approved of such a new and immodest fashion. Hester studied the gloves. Now that they were far away from any prying Moon Street eyes, were they allowed to wear whatever they wished? Could they do what they felt like? These new possibilities both exhilarated and befuddled Hester.

She stood nervously outside the inn door. *What shall I do when I go inside?* Without her sister, she was uncertain how to act. Hester had grown so accustomed to organizing and directing Philena, she didn't know what to do when she was on her own and had no one to boss around or prompt.

"Come now!" Madame Knight hissed from the open doorway at Hester and her daughter. "Do as I say and do not, I repeat, do not speak to anyone until I signal that this is appropriate. Remember, we are among strangers now."

Polly nodded with the great seriousness. Hester gulped and followed her mistresses through the door. The smoky tavern was loud and dark. The place smelled of tobacco and stale ale and sweat. A great fire blazed in the stone fireplace. Men in greasy leather pants leaned against the wall with their large muddy boots outstretched. They smoked long clay pipes and talked and joked and laughed with a heartiness that seemed oddly disconcerting. Other men huddled forward, their whiskered faces hidden in the enormous tankards they cradled with both arms on a long trestle table. No one looked up when Madame Knight and the girls entered.

Fearlessly, Madame Knight sailed around the strangers and the haphazard benches and stools and found the only empty table near a grimy window. She pointed to indicate that the girls should take a seat. Then she slowly lowered herself on to a bench. Polly flicked a greasy rind of pumpkin and a grizzled piece of bone from a stool before she sat down. Madame Knight leaned forward, careful not to soil her precious gloves. She folded her sausage-like fingers together and waited as if she were sitting in a pew at church.

The tavern became completely quiet. The men's heads swiveled. They gazed at the newcomers in astonishment and horror. Madame Knight coughed a nervous cough. She looked at the gawking strangers and said politely, "I understand from the sign that accommodations are six pence for a single meal. A quart of beer is one penny. But why is it that fire and bed, diet and wine and beer between meals is just three shillings a day? Does this not seem unreasonable?"

No one spoke. They only stared.

Hester squirmed and wondered if they should leave. She had never in her life been in a tavern except the one on Moon Street where everyone knew everyone. Here she did not recognize one familiar face. She felt uneasy and anxious. *They are looking at us, judging us.* "How far to the next inn?" she whispered to Madame Knight. "I do not think, Mistress, that we are wanted here."

Madame Knight refused to retreat. She leveled an imperious gaze about the place. "Where is the proprietor so that we might be served? We are hungry and have traveled a long way today." A few of the men sitting close by picked up their tankards, belched, and then edged farther away from Madame Knight and the girls. This behavior only seemed to unnerve the sociable woman more. Her eyes darted here and there.

"Captain Blood," someone murmured.

Madame Knight gave a halfhearted, friendly grin

to no one in particular. Perhaps she thought her charm would somehow convince these strangers to accept her.

"Mother?" Polly whined softly. "Do you not think we should leave?"

Hester drummed her fingers on the greasy table edge. She heard the words again. "Captain Blood," a low voice muttered. The hairs on the back of her neck stood up.

Madame Knight unfolded her gloved hands. She rose to her feet in one surprisingly graceful movement. It was clear that she had decided they would never have dinner unless she took matters into her own hands. "This captain. Where is he? I wish to speak to him and demand service."

Someone chuckled in the shadows. "Can't."

"Why not?" Madame Knight demanded, her voice indignant. "Speak, man. Don't hide thyself like a worm."

Another fellow laughed, though not loudly. "Thou canst not speak to Captain Blood for he cannot speak to thou." A tall, thin man with a leaping Adam's apple jumping about the collar of his shirt stepped into the firelight. He had a spattered apron tied around his waist and carried a mildewed rag.

"Dost thou own this establishment?" Madame Knight asked icily. "Dost thou always treat strangers so badly?"

"Pardon me, madame, but no one ever sits there," the aproned man explained.

Without thinking, Hester took her hands from the table and put them in her lap.

"No meal has been served at that place in years," he continued.

"Why?" Madame Knight demanded.

"Captain Blood's wife, long dead now many years."

Hester gripped her hands together very tightly in her lap. She watched the other strangers pause and lean forward or cock their heads to one side. Everyone in the room was listening.

"When Captain Blood's wife finds someone sitting at that place," the aproned man continued, "she smashes all plates, all dinners set upon that table, small or great, cloth or no." He picked up a dirty tankard and wiped his free hand on his apron.

Madame Knight clucked her tongue. "Nothing more than a preposterous story to terrify travelers. Well, sir, I am not afraid. We came to eat. So serve us and quit your far-fetched tales."

The man in the apron appeared immovable. He scratched his long greasy hair, tied back with a leather string. "Hear me out. This story is true," he said in a serious tone. "Time and again watchers were set near this very place. They were told not to take their eyes from the spot nor take themselves from the room. Yet something always happened."

"What?" Madame Knight demanded. This time her voice did not sound so bold.

"An alarm of fire. A call for help. A summons from the landlord. This but for a single moment, but in that moment eyes were taken away from that table and then *smash! crash!* The dinner was thrown upon the floor, trenchers and spoons and cups scattered and strewn everywhere."

The indignant flush was gone from Madame Knight's cheeks now. She looked pale and flustered. "And so how dost thou know it is a ghost that does this work?"

"What else could it be?" The man shook his head. "Captain Blood many years ago left port with a wife and came home with an angry spirit. That is all we know. She haunted him to an early death, never once giving the poor man the satisfaction of enjoying his ale in peace nor his mutton in quiet."

Hester edged farther away from the table. An icy chill seemed to hover nearby and she had the sudden urge to leap to her feet and run out the door. Somehow her feet were as heavy as iron. She could not move.

"Mama?" Polly whimpered. "I am not hungry. Can we go now?"

"So thou wilt not serve us here?" Madame Knight demanded. "Then we shall move. Girls, let us sit at another table to appease this apparition."

Hester and Polly gladly made their way to new stools, sharing a table with a greasy, bearded man who smelled strongly of ale and tobacco. His nose was bulbous and dark with veins and when he smiled at them his teeth were missing or black in places. Hester gulped. After hearing about Captain Blood and his evil wife, she did not trust anyone in this strange place. As soon as they moved, the hubbub and conversation resumed.

"We shall have the dinner, whatever it may be," Madame Knight told the aproned man, who came to the table and made a quick wipe across the surface. "I am looking for a guide. Dost thou know of anyone from this quaking tribe who might take us to the next station in the morning?"

The man in the apron glanced about the tavern. "Anyone here going toward New Haven who might take this lady along past the swamp?"

"I will pay for services," Madame Knight added.

No one volunteered.

"I will pay double for services," Madame Knight announced. She winced even as she said these words. She did not part easily with her money.

A tankard thumped on their table. "I'll take thou where the Post Road goes," the man with the bulbous nose and bloodshot eyes said. "For a dram of cider and a half a piece of eight."

"John, does your wife know where you're a-going?" the man in the apron demanded. "You aren't supposed to be wandering."

"Don't plague me! I know the way," John replied in a slurred voice. He tipped his tankard back and drained every last drop.

"I'll seal the bargain with a dram," Madame Knight declared. From her belt she untied her pocket containing a small leather bag of coins. She smacked these on the table and indicated to the aproned man that she'd have a dram herself.

In horror Hester and Polly inspected the wobbly new guide. Madame Knight downed the tankard and then carefully wiped her mouth with a dainty handkerchief. When their dinner arrived, it was a cold and bony mass of overcooked fish. Hester nibbled on a piece of hard pumpkin and Indian mixed bread with no butter. Every so often she glanced over at the haunted table and felt relieved that they were as far away as they were from the ghost of Captain Blood's wife.

That evening the innkeeper showed them to their room, one of only a few private chambers in the building. They had to climb up a ladder to a loft while carrying a flickering candle. There was but one tall bed in the small room. It had a feather comforter on it and a thin, worn quilt ragged around the edges. The room was so cold, they could see their breath.

"Now, Mother, how can we sleep in just one bed the three of us?" Polly complained.

" 'Tis better than sharing with a stranger," Madame Knight declared. "We bought a whole bed, not a half. And the inn's full tonight."

"But what of her?" Polly insisted, pointing a haughty finger at Hester. "It will be too crowded in the bed."

Hester stubbornly moved her foot back and forth on the gritty surface of rough, wide pine planks. "There's no spare blanket," she said. "I'll catch a chill sleeping on the floor on such a night as this."

"She's right," Madame Knight said wearily. She climbed with some effort into the bed and removed her shoes. She dropped each one on the floor with a thud. Then she pulled back the coverlet and climbed in wearing all her clothing. "Girl, you can sleep at the edge. But mind that you do not take all the covers from us."

After some effort, they made ready to go to sleep. Polly said her prayers and Madame Knight blew out the candle. Hester lay her head upon the sour-smelling pillow. She lay on her side at the very edge of the sagging bed and stared into the darkness. She thought of Captain Blood's wraith-like wife haunting the floor below them. She sniffed and pulled the ragged edge of the quilt up to her neck and shoulder.

In moments the room rocked with the sound of

Madame Knight's loud snores. Polly, obviously warm and snug in the valleylike middle of the bed, was soon asleep, too. Hester felt cold and wide awake and very alone. This was the first time she had ever slept without her sister. She wondered what Philena was doing at that very moment. *Does she miss me?*

Chapter

4

$\mathcal{S}$aturday—We do not remain long at the Good
Woman to rest ourselves even though my Great weak-
ness requires every Indulgence my dear mother can
afford. I believe I bear my ride beyond anyone's
Expectation but horrid Girl berates me this morning
beyond endurance. My mother says hush Not to pay
her any mind for she is far from her familiar other
Half, namely one twin, and I keep calling her Girl
and this makes her most Upset. "After all these years
do you Know not my Tru name?" she cries. What a
foul-tempered lazy Girl she is not even willing to help
me comb out my hair. Such rebellious carriage! And
she nothing more than an indentured Maid. She's
proms'd faithful Service for the years till her majority

and in the mean time gets housing and keep and Freedom Dues, which she speaks of with such rapture that she makes it sound Like a goodly Fortune. Does she know not she is but a chattel to us? If she were mine servant I would Beet her I tell My mother for her pure insolence. Now she can have no contrivance with her sister and so does vent her spleen on me. Such unnatural Creatures twins are. I am glad I am an only chyld.

The early morning was dark and misty and smelled of wood smoke and coming snow. A small sliver of moon hung low in the sky when Madame Knight, Polly, and Hester awoke. They tried to rouse John, wrapped in a moth-eaten buffalo robe downstairs on the tavern floor before the fire.

"Wake up, sleeping dog!" Madame Knight hissed and poked him with her foot.

"Go away, woman!" John growled. "Let me sleep."

"Thou promised to take us on the road and if thou dost not, thou shall receive no payment."

John swore some oaths and stumbled to his feet. He looked old by firelight. Hester wondered if such an antique man would bear up under a long day's ride. He staggered to the privy where he was gone a very long time before he finally reappeared. By then Madame Knight had instructed the groom to resaddle their horses and make ready their packs for the day ahead. As soon as John swung his leg over his horse's sway back, he headed north.

"Mistress!" Hester called. "He goes back to Boston."

Disgusted, Madame Knight called back John, who was almost asleep in the saddle. Hester gave her drowsy horse a good nudge and they began to follow the muddy path between the trees. An owl hooted somewhere close by, a sign that gave Hester pause. She wondered if it might mean bad luck but said nothing to Madame Knight or to Polly. She had already had an argument with Polly that morning and did not wish to make the peevish girl more disagreeable than she was already.

Hester's stomach growled. She hoped there'd be something for them to eat in the tuck-a-muck when they stopped to rest. But neither John nor Madame Knight seemed interested in lingering along the path. Dew-heavy branches bent low.

Cold water sprinkled Hester's shoulders and head and slid down her neck. *Was there ever such a miserable morning?*

Slowly, the sun began to creep up from the horizon and the sky began to lighten. In silence they ambled single-file. Without warning, John turned precariously in his old saddle tied together with dirty pieces of rope and called to Madame Knight, "What brings you along the Post Road in the autumn of the year with snow soon upon us?"

Madame Knight leaned forward slightly as if to keep herself in readiness in case her horse decided to caper. "I am going to New Haven to settle a family and business matter which may have much bearing on my future prosperity," Madame Knight replied.

Business matter. Future prosperity. When Hester heard these words, her ears pricked up immediately.

"A long, dangerous way for a woman to go alone," John said. He turned and spit into the woods. "You must have a considerable sum waiting for you in New Haven to take such a risk."

Madame Knight did not reply for several moments. "I have my reasons. They are private reasons."

John guffawed. "Don't worry. Shan't tell nobody."

Still, Madame Knight refused to reveal her secret. Instead, she gave her horse a little kick. The horse lumbered forward. The little trunk belonging to Mr. Trowbridge wobbled and jangled as she passed John, who did not seem to realize he'd been snubbed. In a loud voice, he entertained them with tales of adventures and eminent dangers he had escaped. "Once I came upon a catamount and had to wrestle it to the ground and strangle it with my bare hands," John boasted. "Another time I tamed a poisonous snake, then chopped off its head with my knife, all while I was running through the wood so's to escape a wild she-bear about to rip me limb from limb."

"I didn't know but we had met with a hero disguised," Madame Knight said over her shoulder. "Surely the bravest man in all of Massachusetts Bay Colony."

Hester could tell from the tone of her voice that Madame Knight did not believe a word of John's story. Hester liked to tell her sister equally wild tales, but she always made it clear to Philena that they were only make-believe—not true incidents.

Even so, it always amazed Hester how gullible Philena was and how willing she was to pass along tales of Hester's bravery. *Was anyone ever so believing as my sister?* Hester worried that in her absence her sister might be tricked unfairly. It was too easy to impress her.

As they rode on they came to a very thick forest filled with fog. "Beyond this," John warned, "lies a terrible swamp."

"Is there another way around it?" Polly demanded fearfully.

John shook his head.

Hester felt more and more anxious. There were Indians in the woods of western Massachusetts. In the *Boston News Letter* Polly had read aloud stories of people being taken captive. She'd read of massacres. How could Madame Knight have been so foolish? They had no gun and only this silly, weak old man for protection.

Finally, they stopped and dismounted and ate some of the food from the tuck-a-muck. "Do not feel fearful," John announced. He spouted crumbs as he spoke. "I have Universal Knowledge of the woods."

"And what, pray tell, is Universal Knowledge?" Madame Knight demanded as she nibbled daintily.

"It is the great comprehension of all things wild. My grandfather was a woodsman. My father was a woodsman. My brothers were woodsmen. And I am—"

"A great tippler and a great liar," Madame Knight said and remounted her horse. "If you have such a wonderful awareness of the woods, why did we find you in the tavern?"

John put one wobbly foot in his stirrup and swung his other leg over the saddle with great effort. He stared down his bulbous nose at Madame Knight. "One cannot stay in the woods *all* the time."

Polly slapped her reins across her horse's neck and moved closer to Hester's horse. The dark, misty shadows between the stunted pines and thorny bushes seemed to waver like something alive. For the next several hours they wandered along a path filled with briars. The path narrowed, then suddenly ended.

"Where are we?" Madame Knight demanded.

"Lost!" Polly wailed.

John swore loudly. "This way. I know it." He

turned his horse around and they retraced their steps. And for several more hours they zigzagged among cedars and pines. Hester had a sinking feeling that she had already seen these trees before. Her stomach growled and she felt certain they would never find their way out of this forest.

Soon the sun began to set. Ahead a clearing appeared. "Just as I suspected!" John declared. "We're almost there."

They left the forest and came upon a swamp filled with fearsome sounds and strange, disagreeable odors. "Oh, save me!" Hester cried. Her horse struggled up to its knees in thick black mud. She perched ready to jump from the horse into the brambles, certain that at any moment her horse would sink over its head in quicksand. But amazingly, the horse's broad hooves lifted with a terrible sucking sound and she was carried over the sloughy spot.

Ducks and geese flew overhead. Ragged soft cattails shredded and bent as they passed by. The seeds scattered, white and windblown. Hollow stems of dried grasses whispered and bent as a breeze pushed past them. In the brambles Hester spied a pair of red eyes watching her. The musty smell of the swamp rose up all around her and spread a kind of coolness along the ground. The sudden drop in the temperature made her tremble. She wrapped her woolen cloak around her shoulders and longed to sit beside a blazing fire.

"How far?" Polly asked in a hopeless voice. She tried to brush dirt from her cloak. "This mud is terrible. I scorn to be drabbled."

"Not too much farther," John promised. And sure enough, in the distance they saw a lone house with a light burning in the window. The horses began to move more quickly, as if they knew the trail's end was near. John was first to lower himself to the ground. He held his horse's reins as he knocked on the door.

A young, curious woman peeked through a crack. "Law for me," she cried, "what in the world brings you here at this time of night, John?" She opened the door wider and saw Madame Knight and the girls. The woman's neck was long and her eyes bugged out like that of a frog. "I never seen women on the road so dreadful late in all the days of my life. Who are you and where are you going? I'm scared out of my wits. Lawful heart, John! Can't believe it's you. How-de-do! Where in the world are you going with this woman and these girls? Who are they?"

John, stoop-shouldered with weariness, motioned for Madame Knight, Polly, and Hester to dismount. Then he promptly disappeared inside the house without offering to help them unharness or feed their horses.

"Well, there's an ungrateful scoundrel!" Madame Knight grumbled. She carefully lowered herself off the horse and led the tired animal to a falling-down shed. Polly and Hester were too tired to quarrel and followed her.

When they finally came inside the house, they found John sitting by the fireplace making himself very comfortable. From his pocket he dug out a pouch of tobacco for a smoke. Instead of offering Madame Knight a place to sit down or some food, the frog-eyed woman kept talking, asking more silly questions about where they were going and why they were going and when they'd be returning and what did they think they were doing scaring a body so badly in the middle of the night like this?

"Good woman!" Madame Knight said angrily. "I do not think it my duty to answer such unmannerly questions. We have not eaten properly yet today and are nearly famished." She paused and added a bit more kindly, "I have come here to have the post's company with us tomorrow on our journey." She flung off her cloak and carefully removed her gloves. She sat beside the fire. Polly and Hester, not knowing where to leave their muddy cloaks, simply sat upon them on a bench in an exhausted daze.

The young woman seemed impressed by Madame Knight's appearance and air of importance. She ran upstairs and when she returned it was obvious that she had put on jewelry—at least three or four rings and a glittering silver thimble, which she wiggled in the air to make sure everyone noticed. "Would you like to take a seat on the best chair?" she asked and waved her hands before her face. "We have a cold bite of bacon and some biscuit. I can fry the meat for you if you like," she said. Before she prepared the meal, she took off her rings and thimble. "These are nothing. Mere trifles," she announced to no one in particular. "I never pay them much heed." She did not appear to notice when she accidentally knocked the little thimble from the corner of the table. It rolled under Hester's foot.

When she was sure no one was looking, Hester picked up the thimble and, without thinking, tucked it inside her pocket, which hung from a string around her waist. For once, the preacher's threats about sin and Everlasting Punishment never crossed her mind. It was as if their journey along the Post Road had carried them to a place where all familiar rules and consequences no longer applied. She ate her dinner quickly and forgot about the thimble.

"Here is your payment as we agreed," Madame Knight said to John when they were finished with their greasy meal. She gave him his money, which he accepted eagerly. Hester wondered if he had worked for so much in as many months.

"You'll be needing lodging, too, I suppose?" the young woman asked, clearly impressed by the little bag of coins that Madame Knight seemed to distribute so freely.

Madame Knight nodded wearily. The talkative young woman showed them a little room in a back lean-to, which was so small, even the narrow bed nearly filled up the whole room. The bed stood so high that Hester and Polly had to help Madame Knight climb on a chair to reach it. Madame

Knight handed Hester a blanket and she pulled out a pallet that had been tucked under the bed for what must have been many years.

Hester felt as if she were sleeping in a long narrow cave. When she looked up she saw the wall on one side and the side of the tall bed on the other. She shut her eyes and had the terrible sensation that she was falling into deep, black mud. Exhausted, she turned her head on a sad-colored pillow, which she soon discovered was plagued by fleas. The bugs bit her face and neck all night. After many sleepless hours, she remembered the thimble tucked in her pocket and felt strangely pleased to have taken it.

Chapter 5

Since the moment Madame Knight, Polly, and Hester left on their journey, the house on Moon Street had become a regular hurrah's nest. Right away Goodwife Kemble began ordering Philena about as if she were the only crewmember on a full-rigged ship.

"Look lively!" Goodwife Kemble shouted and thumped her cane against the ceiling of the kitchen. The floor beneath Philena's bed gave a loud knock.

Philena sat bolt upright in the cramped, dark loft. Her sister's bed was empty. Her terrible dream was true. *She's gone.* Reluctantly, she dressed and scrambled down the ladder to set the fire and make breakfast.

"I'm captain now," Goodwife Kemble declared. And although it was Saturday, which was the usual day to bake a dozen or more loaves of bread for the week, Goodwife Kemble announced that because the sun was shining and the wind was stark calm, it was a perfect day to do the laundry.

Philena sighed. She hated doing the laundry. It would be an even longer, more hateful job working alone. But she had no choice. Goodwife Kemble was in charge.

At breakfast it seemed very strange not to share a trencher of gruel with Hester. How odd to have her own spoon, her own leathern cup of cider to drink. "There's no use looking so forlorn, Girl," Goodwife Kemble announced. "We've plenty of work to do."

Philena looked up from her breakfast. In all the years of living at Madame Knight's, she could not remember one time that anyone called her Philena. *Why is that?* She stirred the gruel slowly. She quietly said her name aloud just to remind herself. "Phi-len-a," she whispered. It still sounded unfamiliar. *Who's she?*

"What?" Goodwife Kemble asked.

"Nothing," Philena answered. *I'm always Us or*

We. Never Me. But now here she was, all by herself. She looked about the room self-consciously. *She's gone.* Philena felt strange, as if she'd forgotten something important. Her other self. She felt as naked as if she were walking down Moon Street without a proper cap.

The kitchen seemed far too quiet with chatty Polly and Madame Knight gone. *Hester always does the talking for me.* Philena tried to think of something to comment upon. The weather? The work? Philena racked her brain.

Goodwife Kemble nervously tapped her foot as if she were feeling wadgetty, too. "Do not tarry, Girl," she blurted, clearly unable to stand the silence a moment longer. "There is work to be done."

Doing the laundry was a backbreaking job. First Philena had to haul piles of firewood to the yard. Then she had to fill a great kettle with water carried in buckets from the spring. She collected the dirty clothes by the armful. Dark woolen jackets and petticoats went from year to year without seeing a kettle of suds. But there were always plenty of shifts and aprons, handkerchiefs and shirts to wash.

Philena set a great fire burning in the yard and laid a kettle over it. Once the water was boiling good and steady, she added the strong lye soap and carefully dropped in the dirty clothes. She stirred them with a beating staff. Smoke blew in her eyes and made her wince and blink. As best she could, she picked up a soggy, steaming bunch of clothing with the long pole, then plopped them into another washtub of fresh rinse water. She bent over and wrung out the clothes with her hands and hung them on the line to dry. She did not feel like singing. *Who would join me at the chorus?*

Once each item was dry, she collected them from the line or the bush where they hung and carried them into the kitchen. Here she pressed the clothing carefully on the table using smoothing irons fitted into a heater, which she filled with coals from the fire. Ironing was the part of the job she hated most: walking back and forth from hearth to table to hearth again to stoke the heaters that kept the heavy irons warm.

Philena leaned against the table. With one chapped hand, she rubbed her eyes. She wondered what her sister might be doing at this very moment. *Not laundry, certainly.*

Suddenly, Philena felt jealous. What was so difficult about riding a horse? Certainly there were dangers, but at least life did not seem so abominably boring as what she was experiencing. Her back and arms ached. Her hands and wrists were sore. Doing the laundry alone was going to take the better part of two days.

Wearily, she sat down on a stool.

"What are you doing, idle creature?" Goodwife Kemble declared. "I thought you were tending the kitchen halyards."

Philena jumped to her feet. "I was, Mistress. Just resting, Mistress."

Goodwife Kemble sat down wearily. "Ah, me. We can look out for squalls all we can, but they still come upon us unawares."

"Mistress?" Philena asked, wondering if the old woman was feeling ill. "You seem a bit peaked."

"I'm bung up and bilge free, same as usual," Goodwife Kemble declared heartily. "It's my daughter I'm worried about."

"Bad news?" Philena asked anxiously. Her worst fears for Hester flashed before her. *Eaten by a bear. Scalped. Drowned.* "Tell me, please. I must know."

Goodwife Kemble placed her tight fist on the table, palm down. She turned over her hand and opened her knobby fingers. And there lay a curious object. It was shaped like a tiny glittering hoof no bigger than a man's finger from the knuckle to the tip. A leather string had been looped and tied at one end. "What is it?" Philena whispered.

"I've seen sailors carry such potent amulets for good luck. It's a guinea deer's foot dipped in real gold."

Philena dared not touch it or get too close. She knew Goodwife Kemble understood and followed all sailor omens and superstitions. This object clearly unnerved the old woman. Philena did not wish to tempt fate by doing the wrong thing. "Where did it come from?"

"West Africa."

"No, I mean how did it come *here?*"

Goodwife Kemble moaned. "When I was cleaning Mr. Trowbridge's room I decided to turn his mattress. And when I did, I discovered this fallen upon the floor. It must have belonged to him." She added in a sorrowful tone, "Don't you see? We cannot simply keep it or heave it overboard. We must return it with the other possessions, for it is certainly valuable and much too powerful for us to keep."

"Too powerful?" Philena gulped.

"We used to bury such things at sea with a sailor when he died," Goodwife Kemble said in a low voice. "But that's not possible, seeing as how Mr. Trowbridge is seven feet underground."

Philena tapped her finger against her nose to help her think. "We could return it with the other belongings to Mr. Trowbridge's family. In that way, *they'd* have to decide what to do with it."

"How? My daughter already has a day's sail ahead of us."

Philena thought hard. "Cato. We could send Cato. He's a good rider."

"If he clipped along," Goodwife Kemble said, nodding. Then she frowned. "The boy won't make it no matter how fast he goes. Some buccaneer will kidnap him. Or he'll sail off and never come back."

Philena nodded. "You're right."

Goodwife Kemble shook her head and rocked back and forth and cried with confusion. "Oh, my daughter will certainly be angry with me, I know it."

"Now, now," Philena said gently. She hated to see Goodwife Kemble so forlorn. "I could go with Cato," she suggested. The more she thought about it, the more appealing the idea became. *I could see my sister again. I could make sure she's all right.*

Goodwife Kemble seemed to brighten. "You'll make sure he doesn't jump ship."

"I'll be your anchor to windward," Philena said, using Goodwife Kemble's favorite phrase to describe a provision against disaster.

"You're a clever one, Girl," Goodwife Kemble said and smiled. "You must leave immediately. There's not a moment to lose."

Philena grinned. No one had ever called the left hand clever.

Goodwife Kemble handed Philena the guinea deer's foot. "Do not lose it. And as soon as you make the delivery, turn around and come back to port. If you do not return in one day, I shall send the authorities out after the both of you."

Philena made a solemn promise and slipped the deer's foot into her pocket. She quickly wrapped a few pieces of bread and a chunk of cheese in a handkerchief and tucked these in a saddlebag while Cato harnessed the horse. He seemed thrilled to escape from his endless chores. Philena tried to feel brave as she climbed up behind him and held tight to him and the saddle.

"Greasy luck to you!" Goodwife Kemble shouted a whaler's favorite farewell. "Point your bow south toward New Haven. You cannot miss them."

Philena and Cato rode south on the Post Road as fast as the horse would gallop. Their first stop was the Good Woman Tavern. Dirty and tired from riding almost without stopping, Philena felt glad to see a place where they could eat and rest before resuming their journey. She felt sore from bumping along on the horse and looked forward to a hot meal. Goodwife Kemble had entrusted her with a small bag of coins to use to pay for their meals on the way. Cato, too, seemed more than happy to rest.

While he led the horse to be fed and watered, Philena opened the inn door. Once her eyes became accustomed to the lack of light, she walked inside and took a seat at an empty table.

Immediately, all eyes were upon her. She felt the same way she did when she walked among strangers too close beside her sister. Only Hester was not here. She had no one to do the talking for her. She gulped as a tall, sallow-faced man in a dirty apron approached her. His eyes shifted about nervously. "What art thou doing back so soon?" he demanded. "And where is John? I told thou not to eat at this table, and yet thou disregards my advice. Art thou not afeared of ghosts?"

She tried clearing her throat. It took every ounce of courage she had to speak. "I beg thou pardon, sir. I don't know what ghosts thou speaks of. Is one called John?"

The man in the apron leaned closer and gave her a dark look. "Has some misfortune befallen him that thou now calls him a haunt?"

Philena felt confused. "I call him that only because *thou* does."

The man snapped the towel and hit a fly squarely. "Thou art a bold one to come in alone. And what happened to the older noisy woman and her pretty daughter? Have thou done away with them, too?"

"You mean my mistress," Philena said eagerly.

"Yes. That is the one I mean. She lured John away from his own wife and fire. Perhaps you were working together. I have heard of such thieves on the road."

Philena stood up. Her hands were shaking. "When was my mistress here? Yesterday?"

"You play the part of the stupid calf very well," the man with the apron replied. "But thou shalt not get away so easily." He lunged forward as if to grab Philena by her arm. But Philena was too quick. She darted out of his grasp and ran for the open door in terror.

"Trouble?" Cato demanded. He stood outside and was nearly knocked over by her.

"No time to explain," Philena said. "Get the horse."

Cato did as he was told. He jumped onto the horse's back and pulled Philena up behind him. An excellent horseman, he seemed delighted to spur the great horse and gallop away at full speed. They hurried off just as the owner of the tavern came outside and shouted to them to stop. They ignored him and rushed on. Philena held on for dear life. When they reached a forest, Cato slowed the horse to a trot and then to a walk.

Philena's breath came more regularly now. She had been so terrified, her hands were nearly cramped from holding on so tight to the back of Cato's saddle. "We are lucky to have escaped," she said. "That man is quite mad. He wanted to capture me and send me to jail."

"Why?"

"He thought I was a murderer."

"You?" Cato laughed derisively. "Who you murder?"

"It doesn't matter," Philena said and pouted. She did not like to be made fun of, especially by Cato.

"I be careful," he said, grinning over his shoulder. She did not speak to him again until they entered a dark forest.

In the distance they saw someone approaching on a slow horse. The stranger waved at them. "Where to?" the stranger demanded. His flushed face was friendly until he saw Philena. Suddenly, all the color seemed to drain away. "These woods must be haunted or I do need another drink," he said, his voice trembling. "Art thou not the girl I just left many miles away? How did thou get all the way back here and not once pass me on the path? Art thou a spirit?"

Philena smiled. "You must mean my sister. Where did thee see her?"

John seemed too terrified to reply. "Goodnight and farewell and do not follow me, spirit!" he cried and kicked his old horse hard so that it leapt around them and galloped away.

"They must be up ahead not too far," Philena told Cato once they entered the swamp. For the first time, self-assured Cato seemed frightened. "Ancestor spirits," he said and motioned with one hand.

Philena glanced nervously about the misty place. "Are you sure this is the way we should go?" Philena asked.

Cato shrugged. "Only way south," he said and pointed to the sun.

Cato's sense of direction did not make sense to Philena. She had seen other trails wandering off from the main one. What if they had picked the wrong way to go? Meanwhile, Cato skillfully managed to guide and cajole the big horse around the muddy places. Philena felt relieved when at last they came upon a house. "We'll stop here," she said. Her stomach growled and she realized she had not eaten anything since they left Moon Street.

As soon as she knocked on the door, she wished

she hadn't. "You!" a frog-eyed woman screeched. "Thief!"

Philena backed quickly away. Without a word, she scrambled back on the horse. Cato kicked the horse hard, and they were soon rushing into the darkening trees.

Chapter 6

Night was coming and they still had not found Madame Knight, Hester, and Polly. Unwilling to take another chance at an inn where they might be chased away or locked up or worse, Philena wondered if they might be better off resting anywhere they could and then setting off at first light.

"What about Goody?" Cato asked. "She think we run off." He was referring to Goodwife Kemble and her threat to send slave catchers with dogs after them.

"What else can we do? We can't go back until we make the delivery." Deep down, she wanted to see her sister again. She wanted to see for her own eyes that Hester was all right.

Geese soared overhead in the darkening sky. The noisy flock moved like one giant V-shaped bird with slender, trailing wings. Their haunting farewell cries filled the evening and made Philena shiver. The geese were journeying far away. She wondered when she, too, would see her sister or their home again.

"Are there bears in these woods?" Philena asked in a small voice.

Cato shrugged.

"Catamounts?"

He shrugged again. "Maybe wolves, too."

This made Philena feel more nervous than ever. She did not like the idea of traveling in the dark when there might be so many vicious hidden creatures waiting to eat them.

"We stay there," Cato said. He pointed to a dilapidated log house half-hidden by trees.

"Do you think anyone's there?" Philena asked. She looked for signs of smoke coming from a chimney or a light at the windows. The place seemed to be deserted. Wind rattled nearby tree branches. Reluctantly, she agreed to go inside the abandoned shack. She and Cato climbed off the horse. After removing the saddle, Cato hobbled the horse so that it could not wander far as it grazed whatever it could find to eat.

"Hello?" she called as bravely as she could.

An owl hooted and startled her.

She pushed open the rotting wooden door. Something scampered past her foot. She stifled a scream.

"Mouse," Cato said.

The one-room house was no bigger than the keeping-room. The walls, made of half-hewn logs, had great gaps and there was a hole in the ceiling. The place smelled damp and moldy, as if it were slowly becoming part of the forest again.

"See? No one here," Cato declared. He began collecting wood to build a fire in the middle of the room. He took from his pocket two small pieces of flint, which he struck together until he made a spark. Carefully, he blew on the little, smoldering pile of pine needles and dried moss. Soon the fire grew and he added bigger chips of bark and small branches. Smoke rose out the hole in the roof.

Once the flames began to roar, Philena felt safer. *No wild beasts will come close now.* She unpacked their bread and cheese and sat inside the circle of light and warmth with her cloak wrapped around her shoulders.

Cato joined her. He stared into the fire and slowly chewed the bread and cheese. Philena had never had a real conversation with Cato. Her sister usually did all the talking. Even though she had ridden with him all day, they had not really exchanged more than a few words. Now she felt awkward. After several moments of silence, she blurted, "You ride a horse very well."

Cato smiled. "My father teach me."

"Do you ever think about your family? Do you think they wonder where you are?" she asked, surprised how easy it was to think of something to say.

"Always." He poked the fire with a stick.

"You can remember them. You are lucky."

Cato smacked a stick against a smoldering log. Sparks flew. He stared into the fire and scowled. "Lucky, hah!"

Philena had never considered that having a few memories, however scanty, might be worse than having none at all. She and her sister could invent their mother. Cato knew his mother existed, but he could neither see nor hear her. He couldn't visit her. He could only remember. "I am sorry to have made you sad and worried," Philena said.

Cato looked up briefly at her and for a split second, his angry mask seemed to fall away. He was no longer the bragging, joking, defiant Cato. He looked vulnerable and afraid. And then, just as quickly, the mask went up again. "You the one should be worried," he said.

"Why?" Philena asked nervously.

"I hear Mistress say she can't keep two of you no more. She say she go sell your sister's time. That why she make trip."

Philena gulped. "She took my sister to work for somebody else? She's separating us for good?"

He nodded wisely. "She keep good secret, but not from Cato."

Philena was stunned. Suddenly, everything made sense. The hurry. The lies. The promises. Madame Knight had not even told her own mother the truth. *Goodwife Kemble never would allow us to be split apart. Never.* Philena felt sick to her stomach. With every passing moment, her sister was moving farther and farther away from her, never to return.

Cato jabbed the stick in the dirt. "Mistress say she get plenty money."

"We have to find them. I have to warn my sister. I have to stop Madame Knight," Philena said. Her voice sounded high-pitched and frantic. "We must go right away. What if we're too late?"

Cato motioned toward the open doorway and the darkness beyond. "Too dangerous now. Go in morning. Get some sleep." He threw a few more branches on the fire and curled up on the ground with his back to the flames.

He doesn't care. She's not his sister. Philena wrapped herself in her cloak. Her mind raced with terrible possibilities. *What if I never see her again? I never told her I loved her. I never said good-bye.* The dirt floor felt prickly against her shoulder. She tried not to sleep. She had to think of a plan. But her eyelids were so heavy, she closed them. Soon she was asleep. That night she dreamed she was searching for her sister in an enormous, echo-filled house. She called her sister's name over and over in the empty rooms. "Hester-Phina! Hester-Phina!" Her sister never answered.

Philena awoke the next morning exhausted and disturbed. Her cheek was imbedded with a twig and a small pebble. She sat up shivering and brushed the dirt from her face. *Where am I?* The fire had dwindled to glowing ashes. She could see no sunlight through the cracks in the walls and the hole in the roof. Outside the open door swirled damp, cold mist. Everything was quiet.

Too quiet.

"Cato?" she called in a hoarse voice.

No answer.

She scrambled to her feet. "Cato?"

Frantically, she searched the shack, then hurried outside. The horse had vanished. So had Cato.

In disbelief she called to him again and again. Perhaps this was some kind of joke. He liked to play tricks. Perhaps he was hiding, watching her panic, laughing. "Cato!" she called as loud as she could.

Something large and gray flapped noiselessly overhead. Instinctively, she raised her arms to her face and bent double. For several moments, she wasn't sure how long, she crouched on the ground. Her heart pounded.

Finally, she stood up. The owl was gone. Cato was gone, too. She was completely alone. For the first time in her life, she had no one to tell her what to do, what to think, what to say. No one to make the fire. No one to show her the way. Her sister's words echoed in her ears: *a bigger fool than I thought.*

Shocked and confused, she went back inside the shack and kicked a few dry twigs into the ashes. *Perhaps Cato will come back.* The fire smoldered. Wisps of smoke rose. She sat down and watched the feeble flames. She felt inside her pocket. The guinea deer's foot. *Perhaps he went to find something for us to eat. I'll just wait for him.* She watched the flames sputter, then disappear. She did not know what else to do. She sat there a very long time, her knees bent, her arms wrapped around her legs.

And still he did not return.

The sky began to lighten. She was cold and hungry. More geese passed overhead. This time she felt their cries mocked her. *Cato's never coming back.* He had purposefully left her here to make his escape. She wondered how long it would take him to ride to the Carolinas. Although she felt betrayed, she could not blame him.

At last she stood up. *I must find my sister.* She would have to figure out a plan on her own. Slowly, carefully, she wrapped the cloak around her shoulders and lifted the hood over her head.

She knew then that she could no longer stay where she was. She had to hurry and keep moving south on the Post Road. She had to catch up with Madame Knight, Polly, and her sister.

As soon as she began to walk faster, she felt warmer. Mist lingered in the hollow places. Birds chattered. The fragrant path, thick with pine needles, was soft and springy under her feet. She paused to watch a squirrel dash up a tree. And for the first time she realized she was making all her own decisions. She could walk fast or slow, south or north. She could stop or sleep, and no one was there to tell her what to do or how to feel or what to think. To her complete surprise, she began to laugh.

The squirrel seemed to find her behavior very strange and dashed out of sight.

Suddenly, she heard an odd sound behind her. *A bird?* She paused and listened. No, it was a man singing. The words floated between the trees like an enchantment:

> *"One night when the wind it blew cold*
> *Blew bitter across the wild moor,*
> *Young Mary she came with her child*
> *Wand'ring home to her own father's door."*

She bit her lip and wondered what to do next. Goodwife Kemble warned her to be always on deck, ready for anything. *Do Mohawks sing English songs?* What if the fellow had a scalping knife? Or perhaps he was just another traveler. Should she hide? Should she run? Or should she join him? There might be advantages to having a companion while walking through the woods. To scare away wolves and—

"Hello?"

Too late. Philena turned and could see the man coming closer. He wore a black cloak and rode a tall, dark horse. The man gestured to her with a half-eaten apple. "Where art thou going on such a beautiful morning?" he called in a friendly manner. He did not seem the least startled to see another lone traveler so early.

Speechless, she stood looking up at him. Vapor steamed from the horse's nostrils. Instinctively, she took a step back, fearful of being crushed. The stranger halted his horse, leaned forward, and stared down at her. His black, wide-brimmed hat was pulled down so she could not see his eyes. He had no beard. A deep dimple in his chin danced when he chomped another bite of apple.

"I . . . I am seeking my mistress . . ." She could not think of anything else to say. The horse stomped impatiently. She moved to the edge of the path as if to let him pass. But he did not budge.

"Hast thou never observed a passion for going abroad to attend a guilty conscience?" The stranger's voice was melodic and deep. He used the kind of fancy, confusing words Madame Knight sometimes employed, which made her think he must be a man of distinction and learning. "The jolting of a horse and the company of strangers seem to act as opiates upon it."

"Sir?" she said, not understanding a word of what he was saying. She stared at the apple in his gloved fist and licked her lips.

"Art thou hungry?" he asked kindly. His saddle creaked as he reached back and produced from his saddlebag three bright red apples. His hand was so big, he easily held all three apples at the same time.

She took a step gingerly forward toward the steaming, snorting horse and quickly took the apples from him. "Thank thee kindly, sir," she said and bit into one almost immediately. Until that moment, she had almost forgotten how long it had been since she had had something to eat.

He smiled as he watched her eat. With a gloved finger, he pushed back his hat and she could see his eyes. They were careful green eyes that reminded her of a cat. He seemed old, but not as old as Madame Knight. "Traveled far?"

Apple juice dribbled down her chin. Her mouth was too stuffed to speak. She shrugged. The journey had seemed endless. But she could not say how many miles she had gone. She wiped her mouth with the back of her hand. Patiently, he seemed to wait for her to speak. *Say something.* "I left from Moon Street."

"Boston?"

She nodded.

"A fair and amiable city. I have always had a natural tendency to seek seclusion. But Boston is a wonderful town to ramble in. Once a year or thereabouts I like to take an excursion there. Is Moon Street home?"

"My mistress's home," Philena said and felt a sharp pang of homesickness. For the first time, she felt so far away from everything familiar that she wondered if she would ever see her sister or Goodwife Kemble again. Her existence on Moon Street seemed to have taken on a shadowy, unreal quality. She bit into the second apple to make sure she wasn't simply dreaming.

"Thou art a servant with papers?" he asked, not unkindly.

She paused, uncertain how to answer. *Papers?* She had no papers. Goodwife Kemble had warned her what might happen if she were found on the road traveling alone. An indentured servant who had run away. *Locked up.* That was what she had said. *Has he been sent by the authorities already?* She thought of Goodwife Kemble's warning and shivered.

The stranger did not pursue this line of questioning. He seemed to have made up his mind about her. "Perhaps thou would like to travel along with me for company?"

Philena glanced up at him and felt strangely grateful for his kind suggestion. He seemed like an honorable gentleman. "I am in a hurry on an important errand." She took the guinea deer's foot from her pocket to show him. "I must deliver this to Madame Knight." She explained all the particulars about Mr. Trowbridge and his belongings. But she did not tell him the real reason why she was in such a hurry to find her mistress. She did not mention her sister or Cato for fear he might dissuade her from her mission or alert the authorities about a runaway slave.

"It is a beautiful object," the stranger said. He leaned over and took the guinea deer's foot by the string so that it dangled and glimmered.

"Dost thou suppose the gold is real?" she asked.

The stranger chuckled. "I doubt it. But I shall keep this safe until we find thy mistress. Climb up." He slipped the guinea deer's foot into his pocket and extended a strong hand to Philena. Faster than a cat lapping chained lightning, she was pulled up behind him on to the horse and was soon trotting along at a pace much faster than she could walk. *What good luck!* She gripped his smoky-smelling cloak tightly and felt hopeful that soon she would see Hester safe again.

"Sir, what day is it?" she asked as the wind whipped in her face.

"Sunday."

Sunday! Ordinarily, she would be sitting at the meeting house all day in strict observance of the Sabbath. But instead, here she was riding along on a stranger's horse, pursuing her mistress and her sister. Although she had only been away from

Moon Street for a little over a day, so much had already happened that she felt as if she'd been gone for weeks.

"Hold on," the stranger said. The big horse picked up speed and the trees rushed past in a dizzying blur.

Chapter 7

Sunday—We came upon a place called Devil's Foot rock, a ledge with many marks like that of Great Heels walking. It was a curious site because the footprints seemed to vanish at the edge. I asked my Deer mother what could have made such a thing but neither she nor our feeble guide seemed to know. The Foot Rock was named by Indians, says he. And I should not be surprised to find a skull or wampum here and was glad to continue our journey and who should we hear calling to us from behind shouting but the other madeservant. She galloped behind on a strange gentleman's Horse. We were so surprised we nearly plunged to the ground. The man stopped, not without some reluctance. He demanded to have a reward to return the wayward girl who slipped from the saddle before he could catch her. "What reward?" my mother demanded. "She's runaway without papers," he says. And both madeservants begin to wail and cry and cling to each other. "Sir," says my mother, "I thank your for your Kindness to Return her to me. You are a Grifter I can see that." She gave him a few coins to make him go away. He was furious but did her bidding and galloped off. And so now we must travel with both girls on one horse, irritating as they are and my mother quite furious for it is too far to send this other one back and we have lost Cato and the horse. "Oh," says Girl, "he took the deer foot." We don't know what she wails about but its Too Late to call back the Wicked stranger. It is a good thing Mama seldom leaves my Grandmother in charge for look what misfortunes and confusions befall us.

Polly glanced up from her journal at Philena and frowned. They sat at a table at Haven's Tavern, waiting for Madame Knight, who was busy speaking to the innkeeper at his desk near the door. Hester had gone with her.

Miserable Philena tried not to look at Polly. *No one understands. No one listens. Not even Hester-Phina.*

What had begun as a magnificent attempt to save her sister had ended abruptly as her own rescue by Madame Knight.

"You are ruining everything, Girl," Polly grumbled. "You lost my mother's slave, her expensive horse. You cost her money for your own ransom. And because of you, we may not arrive on time."

"Sorry, Mistress," Philena replied. She was glad that Polly did not mention the disappearance of the guinea deer's foot or the stranger's threat. "Thou wilt regret this." She felt cursed enough. How would she ever find a way to keep Madame Knight from separating her from her sister? To make matters worse, her sister was not taking Cato's warning seriously. Her sister's words rang in her ears: *You're too trusting. You believe everyone.*

Meanwhile, at the innkeeper's desk Madame Knight carefully penned a message on pieces of foolscap. It took her several moments to decide upon the reward. When she completed the last line, she gave the piece of paper to the innkeeper to give to the eastward-traveling postrider, who would take the copies with him to post at taverns along the route. "And here's a copy of the notice for the *Boston News Letter* for publication in the next issue," Madame Knight said. She handed the innkeeper another folded piece of paper for the postrider that said:

Five pound Reward. Ran away on Saturday from his mistress in Boston, a Sirranam Indian manslave, named Cato, aged about 14 years old, black short hair, markt upon his breast with the letters SK; has on a black brooadcloth jacket, under that a frize jacket and breeches, a crocus apron, gray yarn stockings and mittens, and speckled neck cloth: speaks good English. Riding good Bay mare.

"Hast thou any news for Madame Sarah Knight?" she inquired of the innkeeper.

He gazed at her with gray, squinting eyes. He seemed to have no age — neither very old nor very young. He tucked a large pinch of snuff inside his cheek and then searched through a box at his desk, heaped high with scraps of paper and nubs of goose quills. "Nothing here," he said.

"Art thou sure there's not a message from some-one called E.C.?" she demanded in a low voice.

She was unaware that Hester, lingering nearby, was intently listening to every word.

The innkeeper shook his head. "Sorry."

"Something must be amiss," she said and sighed. "We have come so far already. We must simply go on and hope for the best."

The innkeeper scratched his stubbly cheek. "Wilt thou be needing a guide? The postrider going west should be here soon."

"Good. In the meantime, we will have something to eat," Madame Knight said, her old decisiveness returning. She turned and saw Hester watching her closely. "What are you staring at?"

"Nothing, Mistress," Hester said in an innocent voice. "I am only very famished." *Something amiss. What does that mean? And who is E.C.?* She followed Madame Knight through the taproom, filled mostly with drinkers. It was nearly two o'clock in the afternoon and dinner, the largest meal of the day, would not be served until three. In a corner they found Philena sitting with her hands folded at a table, keeping a safe distance from Polly.

As Hester came closer, she inspected her twin critically—the way a stranger coming into the tavern might. For the first time she noticed that

Philena's face was smeared with ashes and dirt. Her sleeves were muddy. "You look hard used," Hester hissed in her sister's ear as she sat down. Hester felt embarrassed to sit in public beside someone so filthy who looked exactly like herself.

"I cannot help my appearance," Philena whispered, startled and hurt by this comment. "I slept upon the ground last night in a filthy hovel. I hurried here to rescue you."

Hester did not seem the least impressed. "Rescue me from what?" she demanded in a low voice.

Philena tilted her head in the direction of Madame Knight.

"From our mistress?" Hester said in disbelief.

Philena coughed once.

"Would you two please stop your incessant back and forth?" Polly said in a critical voice. Then she turned to her mother to complain. "Mama, what took you so long? I am about to faint for want of food."

"Be patient, daughter," Madame Knight said in a tired voice. "I am moving as quickly as I can."

Polly sniffed. "Mama, your maidservant smells quite loathsome. Must I sit beside her?"

Madame Knight did not appear to be listening. She was anxiously counting her coins and gazing up at the sign above the bar that read:

**My liquor's good, my measure just,
but honest sirs I will not trust.**

The innkeeper's wife, a walnut-colored, thin woman in a dirty dress, brought something that looked like a piece of twisted cable to the table. She dropped it with a clunk. "They twins?" she asked, motioning with her head toward Hester and Philena.

Before Madame Knight could respond, Hester replied, "I am. She's not."

When Polly laughed, Hester seemed very pleased. Philena wasn't the least bit happy. She blushed and felt small and awkward and neglected. *The left hand again.* Why had she never noticed before how bossy her sister was?

The woman trudged away, looking confused.

"Can't you take a joke?" Hester growled at her sister.

Philena's eyes narrowed. She had also never noticed before how her sister could be quite cruel when it suited her.

Polly pushed the bread toward Hester and said in a friendly voice, "Give it a pull." She and Hester worked together to claw off one stale end.

Philena took a small piece and ate ravenously. *Why won't my sister listen to me?* She watched the other two girls nibbling and giggling and wished that she were home again where her sister considered *her* her best friend — not Polly.

The walnut-colored woman brought a dish of pork and cabbage. She dropped this unceremoniously on the table with a fistful of dirty spoons.

"What's this? The remains of dinner from last night?" Madame Knight demanded. She scooped a bit and held it up to the light from the dim window.

"The sauce is purple," Polly complained.

Hester and Philena inspected the meat closely and discovered that Polly was right. "Woman?" Madame Knight called in a loud, sending voice. "Hast thou made our meal in your dye kettle?"

The innkeeper's wife shuffled over to the table and scowled at them. "Nothing wrong with that pork and cabbage," she murmured. "Thou will be charged whether thou eats it or not."

Philena's stomach roared with hunger. She did not care what color the cabbage was.

"I'll not eat of this," Polly announced and crossed her arms in front of herself.

Philena, worried that the meal would be taken from them because of Polly's complaints, grabbed a spoon as if ready to take a bite.

Madame Knight sighed. She scooped a bit of purplish vegetable on to her spoon. Amazingly, she managed to get a little down. "What cabbage I swallow will surely serve me for a cud tomorrow," Madame Knight grumbled.

Hester gave her sister a secret sideways glance and winked. Philena smiled. In their private jokes they often referred to Madame Knight as Madame Cow.

"What is so amusing?" Polly demanded.

"Nothing," Hester insisted. She could not look at Philena or she'd start laughing, too.

"You are rude," Polly said. "Both of you."

For the first time since she'd been reunited with Hester, Philena felt as if she and her sister might be comrades again. Twin souls invincible.

When the postrider finally arrived, they began their journey toward New Haven again. He barely stopped to change to a fresh horse and seemed not pleased to have a bossy woman and three girls tagging along behind him to the next stop. "I am in a hurry." He glanced at each of them, his eyes filled with doubt. "If you can keep up, I'll take you. If not, you're on your own and God help you."

Philena did not find his manner or speech very comforting. Clearly, he meant to abandon them if they could not keep pace. Hester turned to her sister behind her in the saddle and demanded, "Weren't you afraid to stay all night in that place you described?"

"I did not know I was alone until I awoke. That's when I was fearful," Philena admitted. She looked behind her down the path through the trees. She wondered what had happened to the dark stranger. What if he were following them? "We must think of a plan," she said softly so that Polly, on the horse ahead of them, could not hear. "Madame Knight means to sell you and separate us."

Hester thought about the conversation she had overheard at the last inn. *Maybe there's some truth in what she says.* "Madame Knight seems in a hurry to meet someone," Hester admitted. "She asks for messages from E.C. Who can that be?"

"Maybe someone she plans to be your new master."

Both girls were silent for several moments. "We could run away," Hester said.

Philena thought of Cato. "How far would we get before we were captured? And you know the punishment."

Our remaining time doubled. "We'd be old women before we're free," Hester said slowly.

The horse picked up speed. They bounced along. With every step, they seemed to be carried closer and closer to the moment of separation. Hester pulled on the reins and the horse slowed to a trot. "We could both pretend to be ill. Who wants a sick servant?"

"Madame Knight is no fool," Philena replied. "She can always tell when we're pretending."

"We could simply refuse to be separated. We could put up a terrible fuss. A howling fit."

Philena shook her head. "We tried that already. And you know what will happen if we make Madame Knight mad enough . . ."

"We'll be sent to Virginia." Hester sighed. Their situation seemed hopeless.

"We'll think of something," Philena insisted,

even though deep down she did not feel the least bit confident.

After several miles, they came upon a wide river. Brown water splashed and gurgled past. The postrider stopped, stared for a moment at the swollen current, then kicked his horse. The beast splashed up to its haunches in the water.

"Sir!" Madame Knight called. "We cannot swim."

The impatient postrider gave her a scornful look. "The horses know what to do." He splashed deeper.

"Sir!" she cried again, louder this time. "We must have a proper boat."

"A boat, your ladyship? Where dost thou expect me to find a boat?"

Madame Knight's face turned red with anger. "I appeal to thee as a gentleman. We must have a boat or we cannot cross."

"What about the horses?" he demanded.

"Ferry us across in a proper craft, then herd the animals across," Madame Knight announced.

Polly's horse pawed the ground nervously. Her face looked even paler than usual. Hester and Philena glanced into the current. *How deep?* Philena wondered.

The postrider spit and cursed. He swung his leg off his saddle and tied his horse to a leafless willow. Without saying a word, he stomped upstream through the underbrush.

"Mama, I am glad you are so forthright," Polly murmured in approval.

Madame Knight seemed pleased with herself. "It is a helpful talent for any woman," she said.

Time passed and still the postrider did not return. Hester slid from the saddle to the ground, then held the reins so that her sister could also climb off the horse. Hester glanced about uneasily.

"Do you suppose there might be Indians here?" Philena whispered, saying aloud her sister's very thoughts.

"Do not speak of such things."

"What if he doesn't come back?" Philena replied. "What will become of us?"

"Be quiet," Hester hissed. "Stop plaguing me with your questions. He left his horse. He has to return."

"What if he's been ambushed?"

Suddenly, their horses whinnied. Branches broke. Footsteps crashed through the bushes. *Indians.* Philena froze. Hester squeezed her eyes shut.

Chapter

8

Through the trees appeared the postrider. He trudged along the river with a paddle over his shoulder. In one hand he tugged a rope attached to an ancient canoe. "Here's a boat," he said angrily to Madame Knight.

Madame Knight came closer to the shore to inspect the craft. Water sloshed in the mossy bottom. She sniffed disapprovingly. "Doesn't look seaworthy."

The postrider spit with great vehemence. "It's this or nothing. Get in."

The boat bobbed. Madame Knight clucked her tongue but did not say another word. She lifted the hem of her skirt, extended her hand to the postrider, and stepped cautiously into the dugout.

The boat tipped and teetered. She shrieked. "Sit down!" the postrider barked.

Madame Knight did as she was told. Water splashed in her lap. She sat rigidly upright and gripped the sides of the dugout with both hands. The boat wobbled as the postrider climbed in with the battered paddle. He sat down quickly. The slightest movement caused the craft to buck and plunge. He shoved away from the shore and headed for the opposite side. For once, Madame Knight was speechless. With awkward, choppy strokes, the postrider splashed and paddled the dugout across the river. He leapt out on the opposite side, wet his boots, and cursed loudly. Madame Knight clumsily rose and stumbled to shore. Her dress was so wet, she wrung it out with her hands.

Philena watched nervously as the postrider returned to their side of the river. "Thou art next," he barked at Polly.

Lighter than her mother, Polly slipped into the boat and took a seat. The postrider crossed her without mishap. When he returned, he shouted to Hester and Philena, "Come on. I'm in a hurry. Climb in."

For a moment Hester and Philena stared at each other in panic. "We go together," Hester said.

"Not separately," Philena added.

"The boat won't hold three," the postrider said.

"Then we won't go," Philena insisted. Hester looked surprised. Ordinarily she was the one who made the decisions and talked to strangers.

The postrider swore a string of oaths that were so awful, Philena pressed her palms against her ears. "All right, then. Get in," he grumbled. "Can't weigh together as much as the old she-beast."

They did as they were told. A wave smacked the boat and splashed their faces. By mid-river, cold water sloshed up to their ankles in the bottom of the boat. Hester's teeth chattered. "Will we capsize?" Philena asked, too terrified to move.

"Bail!" the postrider said between clenched teeth. He paddled faster. "Use anything."

Hester and Philena cupped their hands and lifted water out of the boat. Hester used her soggy shoe to scoop more water out of the boat. Philena did the same. The waterlogged boat managed to arrive safely on the opposite shore. Each of the girls held a damp shoe in one hand and jumped to the muddy shore. The postrider tipped the boat to drain it of water. "It's a good thing we know how to work together," Hester told her sister.

Philena nodded. "Two shoes are better than one."

But when Polly saw them standing shoeless in the mud, she laughed loudly. "Look at your stockings!"

Hester and Philena felt chagrined.

"How far to the next stop?" Madame Knight demanded of the postrider when he returned from swimming the horses across the river.

"Four miles," he replied. He adjusted his saddle, tucked his soggy boot into the stirrup, and swung his leg up into the saddle.

"Pray, dost thou know the condition of the rest of the road till we reach that place?" Madame Knight demanded. It took all three girls' great effort to help her climb up on to her horse again.

The postrider scratched his dirty head. "There's a bad river to ride through."

"Another bad river?" Madame Knight asked in a nervous voice.

"So very fierce a horse can sometimes hardly stem it," he said. "But it's narrow. Thou should soon be over it."

Hester gave her sister a terrified glance. She could hardly imagine anything worse than what they had just crossed. Madame Knight and Polly seemed unusually quiet and nervous as well as they rode along into the darkening trees. "Sometimes I see myself drowning," Hester whispered to her sister. "The blackest idea of my approaching fate."

"Don't say that," Philena said. "It's bad luck. We'll think of something." She wished she still had the guinea deer's foot. They needed every bit of luck they could muster.

The path took them again through the woods. Something scrambled past unseen in the shadows. Tree branches creaked in the wind. In the inky blackness the only light came from the dull glow in the western sky and scattered stars overhead. "Can you see or hear our guide?" Hester demanded.

Philena shook her head. The postrider had galloped too far ahead for them to make out his shape or detect the jangling of his horse harness. *Not that he'd be any protection,* Philena decided. As they rode along, every lifeless trunk, every stump looked like a hiding Mohican or a tall, dark rider.

"Sir!" Madame Knight's loud voice made Philena and Hester jump. "Wait for us."

Their horse picked up a dangerously fast pace that made Hester and Philena grip the saddle with both hands as they bumped along. Trees swallowed them and suddenly they found themselves slipping and faltering down a steep hill. "Hold tight!" Hester shouted as she nearly plunged over the top of the horse's head. The horse righted itself and splashed through up to its haunches. Hester and Philena shrieked as the cold, black river swirled around their legs. Philena shut her eyes, certain of a watery death.

As abruptly as the river had appeared, it seemed to disappear. They were suddenly climbing up another hill, dripping and terrified but still alive. "Narragansett country," the postrider called over his shoulder.

"What's *that* supposed to mean?" Polly demanded.

No one knew—least of all Hester or Philena. And in a few moments, the postrider had galloped out of sight again. The path narrowed. Unseen tree branches clawed at their legs as they rode past. Bushes seemed to jump at them from nowhere, tangling their skirts and tearing at their feet. The darkness was terrible. Worse yet, the guide trotted so far ahead, they could no longer even hear the drumming of his horse's hooves.

Philena sensed that Hester was terrified. So was she. *What should we do?* Their exhausted horse seemed about to collapse. Even Madame Knight's mount—the largest of the group—wheezed badly, as if it might expire at any moment.

At last, with much effort, the horses and their weary riders made it to the top of the hill. Finally, they had traveled out of the woods. The night breeze felt warm. "Look!" Polly called. In the distance they could barely see a faint light. This gave them all hope. The moon appeared from behind the clouds. Inspired, Madame Knight happily recited an original poem:

"Fair Cynthia, all the Homage that I may
Unto a Creature, unto thee I pay."

Madame Knight paused, as if she could not think of anything else. Boldly, Hester chimed in to help her:

"In lonesome woods to meet so kind a guide,
to me's more worth than all the world beside."

Madame Knight laughed. "Look above us, girls. See in the night sky the constellation of Gemini? And there—the twin stars of Castor and Pollux."

"And who are they?" Polly demanded. She sounded as if stars were the last thing she wanted to hear about.

"Identical sons of Jupiter, who disguised himself as a swan. Their mother was human, but they were born in a large egg. And when they grew up, Castor and Pollux were inseparable."

"Who was Jupiter?" Hester asked.

"The pagan ancients believed he was the king of the heavens," Madame Knight replied.

"Perhaps my sister and I were born of royalty, too. Just like Castor and Pollux," Hester said in a hopeful voice.

Polly laughed derisively, then turned toward the twins and announced, "Perhaps you also were born in a bird's egg, which may explain why you are so peculiar."

Hester scowled.

"Pay her no mind," Philena whispered. She

liked the story of Castor and Pollux. It seemed a sign—maybe something that meant they should not lose courage.

In the distance a horn sounded. A faraway horse whinnied. "That must be the postrider. He's reached the inn," Madame Knight announced, "and signals for us to hurry. Come now. We must keep on schedule. I cannot miss the appointed hour for this meeting. It may be my one and only chance."

As Madame Knight galloped ahead, an idea fluttered in Philena's head at almost the same time it appeared in Hester's. Neither girl spoke. Neither needed to. What if they were to make sure that Madame Knight never arrived on time with the delivery of her servant for E.C.?

Hester smiled at their brilliance. *If she's too late, the agreement will be cancelled. We will be saved.*

Their horses did not need any urging. They picked up a rolling speed as they hurried down the path toward the stable.

Monday—Mama enjoins it upon me to write more details in my journal of the Events that Happen to

me, of Characters that I converse with, and objects I
see from Day to Day; while I am convinced of the
utility, necessity & importance of this Exercise, yet I
do not have perseverance & patience enough to do it
so Constantly as she does. Will I have the mortifica-
tion a few years hence to read a great deal of my
Childish nonsense? Or shall I have the Pleasure
remarking the many steps I shall have advanced in
taste judgement and knowledge? First I should
describe my travel companions: two Girls who look so
much alike and speak so much alike they are like mirror images were it not for clothes.I have never known
such strange and unnatural girls. One answers for the
other as if she knew words before they came into her
mouth. They laugh at silly things like the Shadow of
Mama upon the wall and they walk arm in arm and
never go out of step with one another. Sometimes they
do not speak but one gives the other a look and then
the receiver smiles as if a message was sent. How can
that be? I know they do not like me yet I try to think
that their Hatefulness is a sure means of Improving
myself. If I were their mother I would have
Abandon'd them too. Here I have only them and
They do not need anyone except each other. On this
journey my journal is my only true friend. The

innkeeper when we arrived saw to our Comfort. She took our damp clothing and offered to make us a meal, tho dinner was long over. But Mama, fearful of upsetting her delicate stomach and giving herself nightmares by eating so late, said that all we needed was chocolate mixed with hot milk. I was hungry and so disappointed, but did not complain tho sorely vexed by the long looks of the other Girls who whispered and made unpleasant remarks I know were about Mama. Their insolence confounds me.

Chapter 9

That evening at the inn near Kingston, Madame Knight received a message from the innkeeper's wife. "A letter delivered by the eastbound post-rider," the woman told her. Madame Knight sat with the three girls at a table in the empty tap-room, finishing their hot milk and chocolate. The girls watched Madame Knight break the waxy seal and unfold the paper. She perched her tiny glasses on the end of her nose, read silently, and smiled.

"What does it say?" Polly demanded.

Hester and Philena exchanged anxious glances.

Her mother refolded the letter and looked up, startled, as if Polly's question took her by surprise. "Nothing," Madame Knight replied.

Polly pursed her lips and let out a great gasp of air. "I saw you reading. Those words were not nothing."

"Nothing for *your* eyes is what I meant," Madame Knight replied and smiled mysteriously. "I'll say this much. We have a change in plans. We must go to New York."

"New York? But Mama, you promised," Polly whined. "You said we'd go to the dressmaker in New Haven. You said you'd buy me new clothes."

"There are dressmakers in New York, too. Now go to bed," Madame Knight said. "We have a long journey ahead of us tomorrow." She twisted the paper, went to the fireplace, and dropped it into the flames.

Hester sighed. *We'll never know what else is written there.* In seconds the letter became ashy, shriveled, and fragile as a dead leaf or a lost dream.

"Mistress, did your letter mention Cato? Was he captured?" Philena asked.

Madame Knight sighed. "No, not yet," she said. "Time for bed, girls."

Reluctantly, the girls did as they were told. They followed the tavern owner to their room — a small area partitioned off from the kitchen by a

few rough boards. The bed was hard and narrow, barely big enough to accommodate plump
Madame Knight. For once Hester was glad she
did not have to share a real bed the way Polly did.
At least her sister did not snore and take up all
the space.

Hester and Philena curled up on the floor atop a
lumpy pallet stuffed with corncobs. Soon Madame
Knight began making noises that sounded like
wind howling down the chimney.

When she was sure that Polly and Madame
Knight were asleep, Philena sat up and nudged
Hester. "We must make sure we never arrive on
time," Hester said. "We'll plan a mutiny before we
reach New York."

"That won't work. We're always outnumbered."
Philena held up three fingers. "Madame Knight,
her guide, and Polly."

Hester frowned. "A diversion then. We'll raise a
false flag. We'll use cannons and surprise the
enemy."

Philena sighed loudly. "What makes you think
you're Long Ben the pirate? He had a privateer
and a crew. What do we have? Nothing." She
emptied her pocket on the bed. Out fell a paper of

pins, a hank of yarn, a favorite shell, and a few coins that were given to her by Goodwife Kemble. Not enough to get them very far. "What do you have that we can use?"

Hester smiled. She was not going to allow her sister's lack of enthusiasm to annoy her. She emptied her pocket. A pinecone, a half-eaten doughnut, a comb. "And this," she said proudly, and pointed to the silver thimble that was worth more than everything they had together.

"Where did you get that?" Philena said suspiciously.

"Found it."

Philena scowled. "Tell me the truth."

"The woman wasn't using it. Didn't even appreciate such a fine thing. Said it was a mere trifle. She said—"

"*Who* said?"

"Don't be so loud," Hester whispered. "You want to wake everyone? The woman on the road—"

"You *stole* it?" Philena could hardly believe her ears. "Stealing is a sin."

Hester picked up the thimble. She tried it on her finger and admired it. "I was going to give it back. Just as soon as we passed her house again."

Philena groaned. These pirate stories had gone to her sister's head. "Whose house? Where does she live?"

"I don't know her name. She's a horrible woman, really. Lives near a swamp. Bulging eyes. She talks too much. She's got the worst fleas in her house I ever saw. Bit me all night." Hester pouted. "I thought you'd like it. I was going to give it to you as a present."

"I don't want it!" Philena exploded. "Look," she said, lowering her voice, "you can't give away something that doesn't belong to you." For a moment, Philena said nothing. She felt as if she were going to be sick. *How can she take such an awful risk?* Then Philena remembered the woman who came out of the house and called her a thief. That had to be the thimble's owner. "Don't you realize that when you do something like this, I can get accused?"

"We share everything," Hester said and smiled. "Even trouble."

Philena groaned and flopped back on the pallet. Her sister was impossible. Absolutely impossible.

"When Madame Knight finds out, you'll be beaten."

"What are you saying? She doesn't beat us. She—"

The bed creaked. "SHSHSH!" Philena sat up and slapped her hand over her sister's mouth. Madame Knight's breathing stopped. Then her snores began again to steadily yip and yap, yip and yap.

"You've got to give it back," Philena hissed in her ear. "You'll go to Hell. You'll burn in everlasting damnation. At this very moment you're—"

Something crashed on the other side of the thin wall that separated their sleeping chamber from the taproom. Hester tore her sister's hand from her mouth. "What's that noise?" Frantically, she tucked the thimble back in her pocket. A man laughed loudly and there was a steady *thud, thud, thud* upon the floor that rattled Hester's and Philena's teeth.

"What?" Madame Knight sat up, fairly shouting. "You can't come in."

"Mama, who is it?" Polly said fearfully. Now she was awake, too. It sounded as if half of the colony of Rhode Island were carousing in the taproom.

Hester bravely tiptoed across the cold, wooden

floor and put her ear against the wall. "What are they saying?" Philena demanded.

"An argument," Hester said. "About where the name Narragansett came from."

"Drunken scholars," Madame Knight said with disgust. "Now we'll never get a wink of peace and quiet."

"Named by Indians," a loud voice exclaimed, "because of a great, high briar. Narragansett means 'bush.' "

"No it don't. The name's from a spring," another fellow replied. "I know right where it is and how cold the temperature is in summer and hot in winter. Narragansett means 'hot and cold.' "

The noisy men thundered as if they were all hitting their fists on the table at the same time.

"Soon they will begin to debate how to make a triangle into a square," Madame Knight grumbled. She was wide awake and furious.

"A toast to you!"

"And to the King!"

There was a great clanging of tankards, then silence.

"Can you give us a song, Philip? Or perhaps a story?"

"I'll tell you one," a gruff voice said. He seemed so close that Hester wondered if perhaps he was leaning his chair back against the wall closest to the bedstead.

"Did you hear about Hannah Duston, the famous American Amazon who stabbed her would-be Indian killers and then brought back ten scalps so she could collect bounty? Ten scalps."

"Did she do it for the money or the glory?"

"I heard Cotton Mather's famous sermon after the execution."

"The execution of the Indians?"

Someone belched.

"No, the execution of Hannah's sister, Elizabeth Emerson. Do you not know of her fame?"

Madame Knight was clearly becoming agitated. "When will they please shut up so that we can sleep?"

"Now, Mama. Don't go out there," Polly pleaded. "Please, Mama. Don't do it. I can't bear the embarrassment."

Hester and Philena were fascinated. Here was something worth watching—Madame Knight in a fisticuffs with the town drunks. Heedless of the danger they were in, the men rattled on and on about the terrible hanging of Hannah Duston's sister, Elizabeth. They described the size of the crowd and the day and the weather and how she was one of the few women in ten years to have such an awful fate, for killing her own children, so she deserved to die. "Could any two sisters be any more unalike?" Philip said in a low baritone. "One a heroine; the other a criminal."

For a few moments, there were no voices, no sounds. Madame Knight sighed and leaned back on her pillow. Perhaps the party had ended.

But just as suddenly as the noise stopped, it began again. In a fury, Madame Knight sat bolt upright. "This is not talk for ears of impressionable young females." She pushed herself out of bed, lit two candles, and began pulling on her dress. Without bothering to remove her nightcap or fasten her shoes, she stomped from the sleeping chamber carrying one candle.

"Mama!" Polly said weakly. "Don't—"

Her protests made no difference. Madame Knight was on a mission. "Sir, will you be silent?" her voice boiled in the next room. Hester nudged Philena with her elbow. They held their breath.

"Will you, I pray, speak with softness? We are weary travelers trying to sleep."

"And we are weary drinkers trying to stay awake," someone replied in a slurred voice. The men laughed.

"What if they punch her?" Polly whispered. "What will we do?"

"I pity the man who tries to lay a hand on your mother," Hester said in a low, amused voice.

"What?" Polly demanded.

"Nothing," Hester said. "Only I am sure you do not wish to become an orphan."

"Like *you?*" Polly replied in a cold voice. She took a small scrap of paper from her journal and handed it to Philena. "Perhaps you might be interested in this."

Philena bit her lip. The paper seemed to have been torn from a newspaper. Her sister leaned over her shoulder. By flickering candle light they read silently:

Likely servant maid's time for nine years to be disposed of. Works well with needle.

For several moments, neither Hester nor Philena spoke. On the other side of the wall they heard the men arguing about their horses. "And can she run?"

"Yes, she can."

"Where did you find this?" Hester demanded. She tried to keep her voice calm. *A likely servant maid . . . to be disposed of.*

Polly raised one eyebrow. "It does sound like one of you, doesn't it? The notice fell from among my mother's papers. I picked it up."

Nervously, Philena scanned the small, mysterious scribbles. *How do we know she's telling the truth?* She wanted to look into her sister's eyes, but she was afraid her expression would betray them both.

"I suppose New York is as good a place as any to sell unexpired time, don't you think?" Polly carefully refolded the paper. She smiled as if everything about their journey suddenly made perfect sense. "I would be telling a lie if I said I will miss you. Either of you."

Hester gulped. "It doesn't say our names. It doesn't mention Madame Knight."

"Dear, ignorant girl! Newspaper advertisements do not give names. No room." Polly smiled her most charming smile, leaned over, and tucked away the piece of paper just as her mother reappeared in the room.

Madame Knight's nightcap sat askew on her head. Her outfit and her expression gave her the same crazy look as old Widow Bumpus, who roamed Moon Street with her cats trailing behind her. She parted the curtains and placed the candle on the windowsill. "I plan to seek revenge the only way I know how," Madame Knight announced. She opened her saddlebag.

"Now, Mama. There's no need for violence. A pistol never solved anything," Polly said in desperation.

"I have no pistol," Madame Knight replied angrily. "But I have something more powerful." She pulled from the saddlebag a small leather-bound commonplace book, a bottle of ink, and her goose quill. She sat on the bed, dipped her pen in the ink, and began scribbling furiously.

"Read it aloud, will you, Mama?" Polly said.

Madame Knight cleared her throat and read:

"I ask thy aid, o potent rum!
To charm these wrangling topers dumb.
Thou hast their giddy brains possessed—

the man confounded with the Beast—
And I, poor I, can get no rest.
Intoxicate them with thy fumes:
Oh, still their tongues till morning comes."

Hester applauded. She gave her sister a jab in the ribs to do likewise. Philena's applause was halfhearted. "Did you go to the hanging?"

"What hanging?" Madame Knight said, looking surprised.

"Elizabeth Emerson's," Philena replied.

"Such events are meant to chastise the wicked," Madame Knight said. Her voice sounded flustered. "You girls must go to sleep. Tomorrow will be a long ride."

Polly lay down on the bed with the pillow over her head to block the noise. Hester did as she was told as well. But Philena could not go back to sleep. She kept thinking about the newspaper notice. *We will be separated forever.*

She tossed and turned. *One a heroine; the other a criminal.* She thought of the stolen silver thimble. If Hester were a criminal, did that mean she was bad, too? The very idea of the gallows made her cringe. *What if they came to take Hester to jail but took me instead?*

"What's the matter?" Hester whispered.

"Nothing," Philena replied. She turned away from her sister so that she could not see her face.

Hester tried to imagine what Philena was thinking. The harder she focused, the more hazy and impossible the task became. For the first time she could not read her sister's troubled thoughts.

Chapter

10

Tuesday—*A great affliction I have met withal by our maid servants; at first reunited on the journey they carried themselfs dutifully as became servants; but since through my mother's forbearance toward them for small faults they have got such a head and gowen so insolent that their carriage toward us especialle myself is insufferable. If I bid them doe a thinge they will bid me to doe it myselfe. If I tell my mother of their behavior towards me, upon examination will denie all they hath done or spoken, so that my dear mother vexed as she is by the speed of our journey knows not how to proceed against them. What trouble and plague to have had two such creatures travelling to contradict and vex me! And oh if my dear Mother would only tell me for what reason we make this dangerous pilgrimage. I am weary of seeing the world and we have not come close to our journey's end.*

Madame Knight was so eager to be off on an early start the next day, she hurried everyone out of bed at three-thirty—so early the moon still shone and so cold that they could see their breath. She told the sleepy girls they were on their way to New London, then on to the Connecticut River to Clinton, Madison, Guilford, Branford. They would travel west along the coast into the colony of Connecticut. "Once we arrive at New Haven," Madame Knight said cheerfully, "we have but three days' journey to New York."

"Three days!" Polly said. "I fear cannot live that long at this pace."

"Hurry now," Madame Knight replied.

"I am so very hungry I will collapse," Polly grumbled.

"No time," Madame Knight said. She ushered Polly, Hester, and Philena out the door. Wearily, they mounted their horses. They were accompanied this time by a French doctor. He was a quiet, short man who wore a fashionable wig and rode a handsome dappled mare. "Good morning, *monsieur*," Madame Knight said in a bright voice.

The doctor lifted one finger to his fine felt hat, but said nothing in reply. As the horses trotted through the darkness, Madame Knight boldly continued her conversation with the doctor. "Did you sleep well?"

"Well enough, *s'il vous plait*," he replied in a haughty tone.

"And what do you think of these most unfortunate Indian wars that plague our colonies?"

"I do not discuss politics so early in the morning. Especially with women," he said.

Madame Knight made a low "harrumph" and trotted along in silence. Hester and Philena were glad for the quiet. They were almost too sleepy to stay atop the horse.

"Mama?" Polly whined. "When shall we stop for breakfast?"

"To think he would not deign discuss politics!" Madame Knight grumbled to no one in particular. "Such a coward! I should ask him about the French and their guns and their friendliness to certain red-skinned barbarians."

"Mama! Do you listen? I am hungry," Polly

insisted. When her mother still did not reply, she announced, "No one pays any attention to me. I should never have come. Never."

"I shall certainly not disagree with that," Hester said in a low voice. Philena giggled.

"What did you say?" Polly demanded.

"Nothing," Hester replied. "Except that your mother says we must travel nearly twenty-two miles—a long way with no tavern to stop beside the long way."

"Twenty-two miles!" Polly exclaimed. And she began to weep, but her mother still did not pay any attention. This only made Polly sob louder.

"What ails you?" Philena called to her, unable to bear the sounds of her distress any longer.

"Everything. Simply everything!" Polly declared. She stripped a twig from a bush as they passed. She flicked it against her horse to make him gallop faster so that she might escape from the maidservants.

"Look at her fly," Hester said dryly.

"You might try to be a bit more pleasant to her," Philena suggested. "Why try her patience? She intends to make our lives more miserable if she can."

"I'm not afraid of her," Hester said.

"You should fear her mother," Philena replied.

"Aren't you the saucy one, full of advice!" Hester replied. "You never were so full of high spirits and big words on Moon Street. This journey has made you bold."

"You're the bold one," Philena said in a low voice. "Bold enough to land us both in jail."

Hester did not reply.

"Sir?" Madame Knight called to the doctor. "Where shall we stop tonight?"

The doctor turned and said over his shoulder, "The house of a man called Mr. Devel."

"Devel!" Madame Knight exclaimed dramatically. "Should we go to the devil to be helped out of our affliction?"

The doctor did not seem to understand Madame Knight's joke and kept trotting along without comment.

"Like the rest of the deluded souls that post to that infernal den, we make all possible speed to this devil's habitation," Madame Knight declared, louder this time.

Still the doctor paid no attention.

Hester sighed. "She's once again composing one

of her interminable poems," she whispered to her sister. "I wish she would be quiet for once and give us all peace."

After a long, exhausting ride, they finally stopped. Mr. Devel's house was a grim log cabin located in a clearing of toppled pine trees. Wearily, the travelers lowered themselves to the ground as two women came out to greet them.

"Sisters," Philena hissed. And sure enough, when Hester looked, she saw that the two old, ugly women were every bit alike. They wore the same pale blue dresses, the same white caps. They parted their gray hair the same and wore the same shoes.

"Like a mirror," Hester whispered.

It was so unusual to see such complete, aged twins that Philena stared, too. *One day will we seem this way?* For the first time she wished she were not a twin so that she would not always have to look at her own plainness everywhere she went.

"Can you please provide us with lodging?" the doctor demanded.

The two old spinsters went to find their father after much coaxing. He hobbled from the house in an ancient coat that hung about his arms like the wings of a bat. His bald head shone in the sunlight. His eyebrows stood like white hedges. "No guests," he declared vehemently. "Absolutely not."

"A bite of bread, perhaps?" the doctor coaxed.

"Off my property!" the old man shouted until his face was nearly purple. He shuffled into his house again with such purpose, Hester feared he might return with a gun. The doctor, Madame Knight, and the girls quickly remounted their horses and hurried down the road.

"Will we ever eat or sleep again?" Polly wailed.

Hester complained, "If I could I would just stop here—"

"And sleep along the roadside," Philena added.

"And have the Indians take your scalp?" Madame Knight chided.

At these words, the girls spurred their horses on. Early in the afternoon they reached the Paukataug River, which was running very high and wild. There was no bridge, no boat, no other way across except by fording.

"I dare not venture to ride through. My courage at best is small," Madame Knight announced. Hester and Philena were not impressed. They suspected their mistress's complaint was intended to display a soft, helpless side to the doctor.

The French doctor was not impressed either. "Well then, *adieu,*" he said and gave a little wave. And in a very ungentlemanly fashion, he crossed the river and left them stranded.

Madame Knight cursed all French men. Her feminine wiles unsuccessful, she angrily stormed up and down the river. "Now what shall we do?" She sat wearily on a stump and stared at the treacherous river. There seemed to be no houses nearby where they might find help. The dark forest of oak and chestnut, hickory and hemlock stretched in all directions.

Hester and Philena climbed down from their horse. "This is our chance," Hester whispered. She held up two fingers. "Now our odds are evenly matched. Two of them and two of us."

Philena smiled. She patted the horse and watched Madame Knight talking to Polly. "What do you suggest?"

"I'll wander downstream. When I don't come back for quite a while, you say you're going to find me. You wander in the same direction, keeping the river on your left. I'll give you a signal when I spot you. Then we'll both remain hidden."

"All night?" Philena asked nervously. *What about wild animals?*

"Here they come. Now, remember. The river on your left. This may be our only chance."

Philena nodded.

"Madame Knight," Hester said, "I'll go downstream. I think I spied some smoke in that direction. Perhaps I can find someone who will help us cross."

Madame Knight gazed at her own badly swollen feet. "Do not wander too far," she warned. "Do not take any chances."

Hester winked at her sister as she disappeared between the trees. Philena sat on a stump and waited. She listened to the wind blowing in the trees. Dried leaves blew into the water and skittered across the surface. They floated downriver like dizzy boats.

As Hester walked, she realized how confusing the woods appeared once she was deep inside them. She heard the river rolling and babbling. *As long as I keep this nearby I cannot lose my way. I'll simply follow it back.* She walked and walked. The light shifted and fell in patterns. From her pocket she took a dried piece of bread and nibbled on it. She shuffled her feet through the dried leaves. A bird called. She paused and looked up. A great black-winged shape flew overhead and called loudly. Suddenly, she felt afraid. The bird seemed to be following her. She walked faster. *My bread. It wants my bread.*

The leaves crackled and whispered under her feet. While she struggled to make her way through the fallen limbs and brambles, the bird soared. She gripped her bread in her fist and dodged around trees.

"CAW! CAW!" the bird taunted. The flapping of its wings seemed to brush against the air like breath, like promises.

Hester threw the bread as far as she could, hoping to make the bird go away, to convince it to stop tormenting her. The bird swooped down, grabbed the crust, and flapped its giant wings and disappeared.

Her heart beat in her throat. She sat down, out of breath. *The river.* She looked to her left, to her right. Was it her imagination, or were the woods becoming darker? She jumped to her feet and listened. She could hear the wind, the branches moving. She could not hear the water. Desperately, she tried to remember how she had arrived at this place. *To the left. The water to my left.*

She shuffled through a thick patch of pine needles and around a great tree toppled on its side. *This way.* She kept walking, listening intently for the sound of the current. *This way.* She tried a new direction, wishing she had tried to remember what the trees looked like when she came into the woods. Everything looked the same. Nothing but trees, stark and spindly, leafless as bones.

Finally, when she could walk no farther, she found a sheltered spot near a hollowed tree and sat down to rest. She was so hungry, so tired, so worried. *Where am I? How will my sister ever find me?* What she needed, she decided, was just a few moments to sleep. Not very long. Just a short nap. Then she would wake up and feel refreshed. She'd know what to do.

Hester curled up in the hollow place beside a great fallen sycamore. She shut her eyes. In a moment, she was fast asleep.

Far away where the road met the river, Philena waited. She sat and watched the place where Hester had disappeared. The space between the trees reminded her of an enormous mouth. She wondered when she should stand up and go into the woods, too. Slowly, the sun began to shift in a low arc. She stood.

"Where is your sister?" Madame Knight demanded. No one had passed along on the road. She was clearly becoming impatient. "She should have returned by now."

"I'll see if I can find her," Philena volunteered.

Madame Knight scowled. She did not seem to think much of this idea. "And then what if you don't come back, either? No, I am too old to go tramping through the trees looking for two of you. Polly?"

Polly sat up and rubbed her eyes. She had been sleeping on her cloak spread out in a patch of grass. "What? Are we crossing?"

"No," Madame Knight said. "I want you to go into the woods and call for the other Girl. Her sister will go with you."

"What happened?" Polly demanded. "Is she lost?"

"I can go alone," Philena said in a nervous voice. *Polly was never part of the plan.* "She doesn't need to come with me."

"Mama, I don't really want to —"

"Enough!" Madame Knight said in exaspera-
tion. "You go with her. Find her and bring her
back. In the meantime, I'll wait here and see if
perhaps someone will come along who can help
us. Do not squander any more time. Go on!"

Chapter

11

Reluctantly, Polly stood and followed Philena into the woods. Philena moved slowly, calling and searching. She hoped that Hester was hiding and watching them. *The river on my left. On my left.* If her sister revealed herself too soon, they'd have to turn around and go back and the delay wouldn't be long enough.

"Can't you move faster?" Polly insisted. "There are too many shadows. I don't like this place."

Philena had to agree. The forest seemed to be growing darker and more menacing by the moment. She tried not to think how frightened she had been traveling with Cato, who seemed to know where he was and what to do. Here she was trying to find her way with Polly, who was of no practical use whatsoever. *Where is she?* "Hello?" Philena called in a loud voice. "Come out, come out wherever you are!"

Polly shuffled along through the dry leaves. "I'm hungry. Let's go back."

"We can't," Philena said, trying to think of some way to stall Polly. "We have to find her, remember? Your mother will just send us in again. I'm sure she's here somewhere. Let's keep walking." She scanned the fallen logs, the trees. Everywhere she looked she thought she saw eyes watching. "Hester-Phina!" she shouted. "Hester-Phina!"

"That's a strange name," Polly said suspiciously. "I never heard you use that before."

"It's special," Philena admitted. "A name we sometimes call each other."

"You call each other the same name? That's odd," Polly said. "Do you like being a twin?"

Philena shrugged. "Sometimes. And what about you? Do you like being an only child?"

Polly broke a branch and stripped away the dead leaves. "Not really. I always wished I could have a sister." She waved the branch as if it were a wand. "Poof! Suddenly, there she'd be."

"I sometimes think I'd like to use a wand like that and make my sister disappear." She blushed and suddenly felt as if she'd betrayed Hester.

Polly giggled. "You're much more amusing without your sister around." She tossed the branch over her shoulder. "What's your other name? Not Hester-Phina. Your real name."

"Philena."

"That has a musical sound to it. Philena. I like it."

Philena felt pleased. No one had ever told her that she was amusing or that her name sounded like a melody. "Hello! Hello!" Philena called. She was surprised that she was enjoying talking to Polly. *Perhaps my sister will stay hidden a little longer.* As soon as she thought this, she felt a little disloyal.

Philena and Polly walked and walked. They found strange marks on the bare trees and patches of long dark hair caught in the bark. Philena pulled a bit of it away, terrified it might belong to her sister, but it was too tough, too black.

"Odd," Polly said. She pointed to a group of pine trees where the bark had been stripped off near the bottom. The exposed wood was light and sticky. "I wonder how that happened."

"Let's keep walking," Philena said nervously. She didn't want to say what she was thinking. *Claw marks.* As they walked, she kept the water on her left. She never let the current leave her sight except when she had to climb over fallen trees or circle boulders. *Where is she?* Suddenly, she began to worry. *What if she's hurt?*

The trees were becoming so filled with shadows it was difficult to see. "Perhaps we should turn back," Polly said.

"We can't. Not yet," Philena insisted. "Hester-Phina!" she shouted, louder this time. "Hester-Phina, where are you?"

In a group of trees to their right they heard the crunch of branches breaking. A large oak creaked. Suddenly, the girls heard an odd drumming sound. *Pock-pock-pock-pock.* Something pelted and bounced against bushes and fallen leaves on the forest floor.

"Sounds like rain," Polly said.

"It's not rain," Philena said, pointing to the ground. "It's acorns."

Branches overhead heaved and shuddered. More acorns tumbled in a great shower of rippling and leaping. And before either girl could move or breathe or blink, a terrifying furry shape clambered down out of the oak tree.

An enormous black bear.

Spellbound, they watched the bear's muscular back move as it climbed surprisingly swiftly to the ground. The black fur rippled. Its enormous pie-pan-size paws moved gracefully down, down. The bark skittered and ripped under the bear's weight and the razor-sharp tugs of its claws. The moment the bear landed on the ground, it noisily crunched and crushed the bed of acorns.

"Run!" Philena squeaked.

Polly took off at a lope. The two girls sped around trees away from the bear. Philena looked over her shoulder. She saw the bear rise up on its haunches and point its tan snout straight up into the air as if it were sniffing the air. And then the bear turned and came down on all fours. In that glimpse, she saw the great black body turn in their direction, its glittering eyes upon them.

Philena did not slow down. Breathlessly, she dodged around fallen limbs, unaware that her skirt was ripped and her sleeve was torn. She did not feel the scratch of a sharp branch against her cheek. She ran without stopping. "Come on!" she shouted to Polly.

One minute Philena looked and saw Polly holding up her long skirt, leaping like a deer. Her terrified face was bright red. Mouth open, she gulped the air and pushed between the brambles, the brown curled ferns, the branches. And then suddenly the next minute she glanced and Polly was nowhere to be seen.

"Help!" she cried. She was several yards back, her skirt and cloak tangled in the brambles.

Philena sped back to her, even though she knew the bear was coming. When she reached Polly, she grabbed the cloak and yanked as hard as she could. The wool ripped. Polly pulled away, cloak in her arms, and kept running. "Come on!"

Finally they could run no more. They staggered slower and slower, out of breath, out of energy. They struggled over the branches, the bushes. They bent over, trying to catch their breath. In that instant they dared to look backward —

And saw that the bear had vanished.

Philena's heart beat so loudly, she could hear nothing else. Her ears drummed with the sound and she felt as if she might be sick. Her throat was raw and her legs began to shake. She listened for the sound of the bear. She watched the trees for its great hulking shape to reappear.

"Where . . . is . . . he?" Polly asked with a croaking voice. She, too, struggled to breathe.

"Maybe scared away," Philena said. She coughed. Her thirst made it nearly impossible to swallow. *Water.* She looked to the left, then to the right and felt a rising sense of panic. "The river!" she said. "We've lost the river."

"How do you lose a river?" Polly demanded. She wiped sweat from her forehead.

"The water led our way back," Philena said. "Now which way do we go?"

They looked in every direction. In the growing murky darkness, there seemed to be no north or south, no east or west. Polly bit her lip and blinked hard. "We're lost."

After much discussion, they decided not to wander any farther. *The bear.* They never mentioned the word, they only thought of it. Lumbering along at several hundred pounds, following them. "We'll just stay here," said Philena, who wished she knew how to build a fire the way Cato had. A fire would be a comfort.

"What if we hear a noise?" Polly asked.

"We'll climb a tree."

Polly nervously cleared her throat. "The bear climbed a tree, too, you know."

"We'll take turns and listen for him," Philena said. "I'm sure he won't come back."

That night neither of them slept. The ground was cold and damp. They wrapped themselves in their cloaks and covered themselves with pine needles, leaves—anything they could find. Polly listened to the terrifying murmurs and shrieks and calls of the woods. Philena strained her ears for the sound of her sister. She prayed that somewhere in the darkness, Hester was still alive.

It was the sound of howling early the next morning before dawn that startled Philena and Polly into sudden wakefulness. As if from nowhere, a pack of dogs bayed. The ground rumbled. Men's voices echoed through the trees. Terrified, Philena jumped to her feet in time to see lights bob and disappear.

"Someone's coming!" Polly said in a hoarse voice.

"Hello!" Philena shouted. "Over here!"

The sound of the dogs grew louder. There

seemed to be hundreds of them yelping and howling and barking. As they came closer, the sound became more and more deafening. The girls heard men shouting and cursing at the animals as if to hold them back. Philena wondered if their rescuers might also be their own undoing. She had an undeniable urge to climb a tree, just to make sure the dogs didn't tear them to pieces.

"Hello! We're here!" Polly called, tears streaming down her face.

The men shouted back. In moments, they arrived. The dogs leapt and jumped and had to be tied up with long pieces of rope. "You the lost ones?" a man asked in a gruff voice.

"Your mother sent us."

Polly babbled furiously as they wrapped a blanket around her shoulders. She told them about the bear. About how they had run. Only Philena was silent. "Have you found another girl in the woods?" she asked.

The man holding the lantern scratched his head. "Sent out a couple of search parties."

"She's about the same size as me. Looks the same, too," Philena said slowly.

"Maybe she's back at the river crossing. Let's go

see. There's others out in the woods looking. Lucky thing nobody mistook you for slaves."

One of the men laughed. "That's our usual job."

"Where's my mother?" Polly demanded.

"Right this way, Miss. She's probably worried sick."

Philena and Polly followed the men through the shadows for what seemed forever. As they walked along, the men joked and laughed and did not seem the least tired. Philena felt as if she might never find her way out of these trees again. With tremendous relief, she saw a clearing ahead filled with faint morning sunshine. She staggered toward the light, anxious yet terrified. *What if she's not there?*

Polly broke through the trees first and ran to her mother. Her mother embraced her and all the men cheered. Philena looked everywhere among the half a dozen or so men and sniffing dogs. They had built a fire and were standing around smoking and spitting and talking. *Where is she?*

"Hester-Phina!" a voice called. Joyfully, Philena turned in time to see the familiar face of her sister. She ran to embrace her—just to make sure she was really there, really standing before her.

"What happened?"

"Fell asleep. Your face!"

"Are you all right?"

"Girl, that's enough lag-last and shiftless!" Madame Knight boomed. Hester and Philena froze. "Thanks to these kind gentlemen, we shall be able to continue on our journey to New York."

Hester and Philena clung to each other with a sense of unspeakable sadness and disappointment. Whatever they had risked was not enough. In the end, they would be separated.

"Come along now. Have something to eat and we will cross this river on a boat brought here especially for our use," Madame Knight said in a voice loud enough for a gentleman standing beside the river to hear. He bowed. Then Madame Knight turned to the twins. She gave each of them a hard, cold stare. "You can see you have caused commotion enough. Until we reach our destination, I shall keep better watch over you."

Chapter

12

*Friday—Days pass and I still dream of black bears.
When I try to speak to Phelina she seems to avoid me.
She has her sister now I suppose. Tomorrow we meet
the man that Mama has travelled so fast and so far to
meet. We have hurried through New Haven,
Stratford, Fairfield and New Rochelle so quickly I
have scarce had time to write here. Yester day we met
a man and his daughter traveling to New York. They
give us company part of the way. I am pleased to hear
this because we have heard rumors of a clever, ghost-
like bandit who has been robbing taverns along the
route. At three-o'clock the man comes with not one
but two daughters about 19 years old, each on a sorry
lean jade with only a bag under each for a pillow.*

The girls have such jaded faces. When they spy our maidservants they notice their Sameness and ask rudely: "Are you twins? Which one of you did your mother love best?" And of course when the Girls reply that they have no mother, the two travelers whose names are Jemima and Deborah, crow with Glee. "Only animals have broods in big numbers." And for the rest of the journey to the ford neither Girl speaks to the other, as if to distance themselves and pretend they are not what they are. The trail is rough and treacherous. Jemima makes sour faces and calls to her father, "Oh lawful heart! This bare mare hurts me. I'm direful sore I vow." But the man doesn't stop or slow or listen. He laughs and says the horse served her mother fine. And the girls says "I don't care how Mother used to do." He gives the horse a Hard Slap and laughs and that makes it jolt her ten times harder.

At the Harlem River crossing the horses bucked and whinnied as they were loaded onto the flatbed boat. Snowflakes stuck to Hester's eyes, and Philena's cape flapped as they climbed aboard the rocking ferry. The ferryman seemed to watch the sudden change in weather with a wary eye.

"Hurry up!" he shouted. "Stay in the middle together and do not move about."

Hester and her sister wondered if they'd make it across. Their confidence was not bolstered when they observed Polly saying a frantic prayer. The half a dozen oarsmen put their backs to the wind and seemed to pull with all their might, but the ferry made little progress.

Hester felt at any moment that she might be sick. The cold, gray water slapped up against the boat and with every movement of the waves, the horses seemed to become more excitable. The thumping of the hooves and the crashing water only made the craft seem that much more fragile. Finally, one of the passengers was clearheaded enough to tie strips of rags around the horses' eyes so that they could not see the great roiling river, and that seemed to calm them. Philena gripped the railing and stood beside her sister, trying to keep her eye on the gray horizon of the opposite shore.

"Few more days and she'll freeze!" the ferry-man called.

Philena's face was so cold, she wondered if her eyelashes would freeze together. The wind lashed against their bodies and tangled their cloaks. There was a terrible lurch. Without meaning to, Philena screamed. She stumbled against her sister. "We're here," Hester shouted in her ear over the wind. "We made it."

The ferryman threw a rope to shore and lowered a plank to lead the horses across. "We won't go over again today," he said to one of the oarsmen. The snow was coming down faster and heavier now. They could barely see the opening in the trees where the Post Road continued. "Which way to the home of Edward Cook?" Madam Knight shouted to the ferryman.

He waved his arm. "That way. Follow the road. You cannot mistake the place. The biggest on the street."

"Girls!" Madame Knight announced in a loud voice. Her face was bright red and she held her cloak around her with some difficulty. "We have not far to go."

Hester's and Philena's teeth were chattering as they once again climbed atop the great horse. Polly was too cold, too frozen to move nimbly and had to be helped into the saddle by another ferry passenger. "Good-bye!" she called to Jemima and

Deborah and their father as they went their separate ways.

"Good-bye!" the two girls called back.

Hester and Philena did not wave or say farewell. Yet they felt glad to see the insulting strangers go. "Don't pay them any mind," Philena shouted in her sister's ear. Even so, their comments had hurt her feelings. She was not an animal. Neither was her sister. *Why did they say such things?*

New York, smaller than Boston, had houses made of brick in many colors. Sleighs whizzed past at great speed down the snowy streets. As Hester and Philena's horse walked along they noticed the language the people spoke seemed unfamiliar. "Dutch," Madame Knight said and sniffed.

The muddy, rutted road was slick and icy and the snow churned the way black and treacherous. The horses slipped and skittered. Philena and Hester were glad to see the great pillared house made of bricks. "That must be the house," Madame Knight said. A groomsman appeared to take their horses once they arrived. Madame Knight shook the snow from her hood, adjusted her purple gloves, and rapped on the great white door. The door opened.

A pale-faced maid appeared in the crack. "Your name?" she inquired.

Madame Knight stood up very straight, very tall. "Madame Sarah Knight. Please tell Mr. Cook I have arrived."

"He is expecting you. Right this way," the maid said. She opened the door wide enough so that they could spy the great fire burning in the parlor. The house smelled of hot cider and fine bayberry candles. But as soon as the maid took one look at the three girls, she paused, as if to prevent them from stepping on the shining, spotless floor. "Your servants?"

"These two," Madame Knight said, pointing to Hester and Philena. "This," she added proudly, "is my daughter, Polly."

"Separate entrance for servants is in back," the maid replied. She pointed. Just as she was about to push the twins outside and shut the door, leaving Hester and Philena shivering on the front steps, Madame Knight stopped her.

"Mr. Cook wants to make sure they don't run off. I think it would be best if you took them around yourself," Madame Knight suggested.

Hester and Philena looked at each other in

desperation and dread. The maid opened an umbrella and waved angrily with her hand. "This way," she said. The maid rounded the corner quickly and pointed to a set of icy steps that led down to a door to the cellar. She knocked as loud as she could. No one answered. She knocked again.

The door swung open. An even more unpleasant-looking woman answered. "What you doing coming in this way?"

"Servants. A special delivery for Mr. Cook," the upstairs maid replied. She gave Hester and Philena a shove inside. She made her way quickly through the kitchen and back upstairs again.

Their entrance and introduction clearly came as a surprise to the other servants. "Come in already," a woman seated at the table replied angrily. "And shut the door!"

Quickly, Hester and Philena entered and shook the snow from their cloaks. They stomped their feet. For several moments, they blinked, trying to adjust their eyes to the lack of light. A fire burned in what appeared a great fireplace of a kitchen. At a table sat four unhappy-looking women and a man eating something from trenchers. When they looked up at Hester and Philena, they neither greeted them nor smiled.

"We're traveling from Boston," Hester said. She had a sinking feeling in her stomach. *Is this where I will spend the next nine years?* "My name is Hester and this is—"

"Bad weather to come so far," one woman interrupted.

"How long does it take to ride here from Boston?" another inquired.

Hester nudged her sister. "Five days, I suspect," Philena said in a small voice.

"On horseback," Hester added.

"Why, really, I was never on a horse so long in my life!" the woman replied. "But then, of course, I'm already here."

The other servants nodded as if what their companion had just said made perfect sense. Hester looked at her sister in confusion. Snow melted around their soggy boots, but no one invited them inside or moved to take their damp cloaks or offered to give them anything to eat. Hester signaled to her sister. They took off their cloaks and hung them on pegs on the wall. Cautiously, they moved toward the fire.

"Don't block the warmth from the rest of us," a man said, slopping soup into his mouth.

Hester moved over a few inches. "And so, how is the work here?" Philena asked.

Two women looked up with blank faces. "All right if you can stand hard labor," one said. The other smiled as if she were very clever.

"Mr. Cook's not so bad," another said in a surprisingly loud voice. "He's got his good days."

"One or two," a woman said and laughed.

Hester and Philena flinched. In Madame Knight's home, they ate with the family and the other boarders. They shared the same food and slept upstairs in the same room with everyone else. Only Cato slept in the barn. This house was different. The servants seemed to have a completely separate existence.

Hester gazed about the kitchen cellar and noticed how cold and damp it was, even with the fire going. The floor was made of bricks and the plastered walls were cracked. She supposed that upstairs must be far grander than this. And suddenly she wondered what Polly and Madame Knight were doing. *Having a fine time.* Her stomach growled.

A small bell rang above the fireplace. "They probably wants tea," the slovenly maid at the table said. "Priscilla, you gets it."

The younger woman beside her shuffled off to fill a tray with a pot and hot water. She dumped a few pieces of gingerbread on a china plate. Philena licked her lips. "Not for the help," the young woman with the tray said and sneered.

Philena lowered herself onto the bench.

"Pray, may we have some soup?" Hester asked when she noticed how faint her sister appeared. "We've been riding all day and just had a bad crossing on the river. Nothing to eat since early daylight."

"Well, aren't you fine! 'Pray may we have some,'" the woman at the table repeated and laughed. "Such fine Boston talk don't impress us."

"Give them something to eat," the man at the table growled. "They'd do the same for you."

"I ain't never been to Boston and I ain't going," the servant at the table complained. But she got up and filled two cracked bowls with pea soup and thumped them on the table. Eagerly, Hester and Philena took their places and ate every last drop.

"You look to be exactly the same," the man said, gazing at them suspiciously. "Anyone ever told you that before?"

"Never," Hester said with a perfectly straight face.

The woman looked confused. While she seemed to ponder Hester's comment, Hester slipped from the table and filled her bowl and her sister's with more soup.

"You hear about the jewel thief along the road from Boston?" the man asked. "Amazing things we've heard."

"Do tell."

Philena finished the last of the soup, which had been decorated with only a few pieces of grizzled ham. She pushed her bowl toward her sister and winked. "See here, my lass, can't you get me some more ham? These here are a day's sail apart." Just saying Goodwife Kemble's favorite phrase made Philena feel homesick for Moon Street.

"This thief changes shape. He runs off and nobody can catch him."

"Might be a woman," his companion interrupted.

"Might be. As I said," he continued in a perturbed voice, "this is a thief that changes shape. Flies down the road and nobody sees him coming or going. Been known to leap a roof and they say he's got a helper. A small dwarf man on a big bay horse."

"Good way to make a bit of money if you don't get hung first," the maid said in a wise voice.

The servants nodded in agreement.

Hester and Philena squirmed.

That evening very late the girls decided they could not stay at Mr. Cook's home. While they heard snoring in the maids' quarters, they crept down the steps through the kitchen. They did not know where they would go or what they would do. They only knew that they could not remain in such an unhappy house.

A small fire burned in the kitchen fireplace. They hurried into their cloaks. An old woman sat in a chair by the door, her sewing in her lap. She was asleep.

Hester and Philena walked on tiptoe. Just as they were about to pass, the woman's eyes fluttered open. "Where do you think you're going?"

"For air," Hester said quickly.

"It's freezing out there."

"Let us pass," Philena whispered. "We can make it worth your while."

"How?"

Philena nudged her sister. From her pocket, Hester produced the thimble. "Take it and let us go. Don't say you saw us or anything else."

The woman snatched the thimble from Hester's hand. Philena opened the door and they both quickly walked up the cellar steps. They hurried around to the front of the house.

Before they made it to the street, a man's voice called to them. "Hester and Philena?"

Stunned, they stopped and turned. *Who knows our names?*

Long windows were lit up from the inside. They saw the silhouette of a man on the porch. He seemed to be emptying his pipe. "Come back in here," he demanded.

Mr. Cook.

For one second they considered bolting away down the snowy street. But they knew there was no escape. He opened the front door and motioned for them to come inside.

Chapter 13

As Hester and Philena trudged closer to the house, they scarcely dared to look up at Mr. Cook. He made a little bow as he held open the door for them. His fashionable, curled white wig did not match his dark, jumping eyebrows. "Thou art the servants of Madame Knight?"

They nodded, surprised by this question. "We are," Hester declared in her bravest voice. "And we won't be separated. If I go, she goes." The girls stepped past Mr. Cook into the grand hallway.

He examined them with some amusement. "This way. Madame Knight and Polly are in the library."

Madame Knight and Polly! These were the last

people Hester or Philena wanted to see. Their footsteps echoed across shining wooden floors as they walked past a ticking clock. A great looking glass stood on one wall. Hester and Philena briefly glimpsed their double, startled reflections as they hurried past. Mr. Cook walked quickly. He opened an enormous door and motioned for them to come inside. One wall was lined with books, more books than Hester or Philena had ever seen before in one place. On a large table Hester recognized the trunk belonging to Mr. Trowbridge.

Madame Knight and Polly, wearing fine clothes, looked uncomfortable as they sat in fancy chairs. They seemed surprised to see Hester and Philena. "Mr. Cook, why, may I ask, are my servants joining us now?" Madame Knight demanded.

Mr. Cook smiled in a charming manner. "I have decided that this is a good time to inform thee of why I have made this invitation."

Madame Knight seemed to perk up considerably. Polly leaned forward in anticipation. Hester and Philena kept their eyes on their hands folded in their laps. They listened to the clock tick. The steady noise only filled them with more dread.

Mr. Cook sat down and unfolded some papers. "You have come into some money, I am pleased to inform you," he said. As he read, he tapped one long bony finger on the gleaming desk. "As executor of the estate, I am responsible to inform you."

Madame Knight smiled victoriously. "Wonderful news! I have many things I need for my home and for my daughter. You can see she is a fine girl. A girl worthy of the best."

Polly beamed.

Mr. Cook looked up. His brow furrowed so that his expensive wig moved slightly, like a curled white cat shifting on its perch. "I am afraid that I must make clear for whom the money is intended. It is for the twin daughters of David White, recently deceased. These are the twins I spoke of in my letter, do you recall?" He stared at Hester and Philena. "The amount is fifty pounds."

"Fifty pounds!" Madame Knight said, gasping.

Hester and Philena could scarcely believe what he was saying. *Daughters of David White?* They had never heard that name before in all their lives.

"There must be some mistake," Madame Knight insisted. Her face turned bright red. "What of Mr.

Trowbridge? What of our long hours spent caring for him? What of the danger we exposed ourselves to bringing his only earthly possessions to thee." She gestured to the trunk. She paused and shot Hester and Philena an accusing glance. "I expected the family to be grateful—"

Mr. Cook raised his hand as if to stop the torrent of words pouring from Madame Knight's mouth. "Madame, I do not understand what thou speaks of. In my letter I asked thee to bring along the daughters of Mr. White, if they were still in your employ. I told thee to do this in complete secrecy at an appointed time. This thou hast accomplished with admirable punctuality."

"I always follow the letter of the law," Madame Knight announced. Only the quaver in her voice revealed that she was not speaking the complete truth. She had set out on her journey with only one of the twins.

Philena did not pay any attention to Madame Knight's obvious anxiety. She was too busy feeling relieved. *There is no sale of time. No advertisement for either of us.*

Hester glanced quickly at Polly, whose face had turned bright red. Polly wrapped and unwrapped her dress sash around her finger. She refused to look at either Hester or Philena.

Hester wondered what Polly might be thinking. *No great fortune. No dressmakers, no parties, no marvelous wardrobe purchases.* Polly blinked hard as if she might burst into tears. For the first time, Hester felt sorry for her.

Mr. Cook cleared his throat. "My client, Mr. White, was the father of the twins. Their mother, Sally Pierce, was a single woman from Haverhill, Massachusetts."

Our mother. She has a name. Philena did not need to look at Hester. She did not need to say a word. She knew they were thinking the same thing.

"She is dead?" Hester asked and bit her lip.

Mr. Cook nodded solemnly. "Thou were born May the eighth, 1692," Mr. Cook said, glancing at the paper on his desk. "She died a year later. We have no other details about her."

No details. Philena sighed. She wanted to know what Sally Pierce looked like. How old was she? What did her voice sound like? Was she happy?

"All that we know," Mr. Cook continued, "is that after she died, the twins were given briefly into the care of Goodwife Miller of Haverhill, who in turn gave the infants to the city fathers to take care of when she became ill. And that was how Hester and Philena came under the care and protection of Madame Knight as indentured servants."

"I did the hard work," Madame Knight said in a stunned voice. "I raised them. The money should be mine."

Mr. Cook raised his hand as if to silence her. "When the twins were born, Sally Pierce declared Mr. White, a wealthy merchant, the father. Mr. White was already married. My client contested the claim in court, as was the custom. He won. However, before he died last year, he secretly added to his will that he would bequeath some money to the twins' welfare, if they were still alive by their twelfth year. It has taken me this long to find the girls, whom I discovered were in thy employ. You must understand that my job was secret. No one was to know. Mr. White did not wish to offend his family or surviving legitimate children."

Madame Knight seemed too shocked to respond. "I took them in," she said in a confused voice. "They are very much alive. Sometimes a bit *too* alive, if thou asks me."

Bewildered, Hester and Philena, not knowing what else to do, stood and gave a little curtsy. The information overwhelmed them. Not only had they discovered that they had a mother, they had a father, too.

"I was, of course, glad to find thee in Boston. My search took nearly twelve months." Mr. Cook busily tidied up his papers. "Now thou canst see why this information must remain secret."

Madame Knight did not look pleased that their meeting had clearly ended. "Sir, I have come a long way at considerable expense to bring these two unfortunate girls here. I am not a wealthy woman. In the process of this journey, I have spent a great deal of money on our housing and food and fees for guides. I have lost a valuable slave, a fine bay horse, and much time away from my business."

Mr. Cook rubbed his temples with the tips of his pale fingers. "Mr. White also instructed me to provide a small sum for the caregiver. Naturally, he did not know who that would be. It is not much, but perhaps it will assist you on your return home to Boston."

Hester and Philena looked at the leather pouch

of coins he pulled from the drawer of his desk. "But what of our separation, sir?" Hester asked. "What of the sale of our time?"

"My instructions do not mention anything about that," Mr. Cook said. "Since you are only twelve years old, I suppose you will remain in the employ of Madame Knight."

"Sir," Philena asked, her voice trembling, "might we still be split apart and sent to different households?" She glanced at her sister. "We don't always get along, true enough. But we shall always be sisters. A special sort of bond. That will never change."

"We wish to stay together," Hester said. "And Moon Street is the only home we know. What we want to know, sir, can our time as maidservants be sold separately?"

Mr. Cook rubbed his chin. He shuffled his papers, pausing every now and again to read something. "I find nothing here about that subject."

Hester glanced at Madame Knight, who gave a disappointed sigh. *What we want isn't the money.* Hester looked at her sister and arched one eyebrow.

Philena coughed once. Then she smiled.

"What if, sir, we give the fifty pounds to our mistress?" Hester said slowly. "And then she signs a paper saying she won't separate us—not until we're grown. And we can stay at Moon Street. Is that possible? Can thou write that?"

"An unusual request," Mr. Cook said, "though the money belongs to thee to do as thou pleases." He turned to Madame Knight. "Would you sign such an agreement?"

Madame Knight beamed. She nodded. For once, she seemed speechless.

"One moment," Philena said, raising one finger to her lips. "Not quite fifty pounds she'll receive. But almost."

"What do you mean?" Mr. Cook asked. Madame Knight squirmed uncomfortably.

Hester smiled. "We have another debt to repay."

"How much?" Mr. Cook asked, pen poised above his paper.

"The cost of a returned silver thimble," Hester replied.

Madame Knight looked visibly relieved.

"I also almost forgot something," Mr. Cook

admitted. He pulled out a small, smudged piece of paper folded carefully into a square. He looked at Hester and Philena. "These belong to thee. No reason for me to keep them anymore."

When he unfolded the square of paper, two small, faded ribbons fell on to the desk. One ribbon was green, the other yellow. Each were tied in a tiny bow.

"What are they?" Hester whispered.

"From Goodwife Miller. Her husband saved these and gave them to me when I interviewed him during my search for thee. I believe Goodwife Miller did attach one to each of thee to tell thee apart. Perhaps these ribbons came to her from thy mother. I do not know for certain."

From thy mother. Curiously, Hester and Philena inspected the precious, faded ribbons—their only real connection with the mysterious Goodwife Miller or the woman called Sally Pierce.

"May eighth is our birthday," Philena said in a hushed voice.

"Now at last we know," Hester replied, smiling.

"Mr. Cook, please draw up the necessary papers. I will sign whatever needs my signature. If our business is finished, we will be on our way tomorrow," Madame Knight said. "My tender mother awaits our return in Boston."

Mr. Cook cleared his throat. For the first time, he seemed nervous. "I would hope I might persuade thee to stay a day longer. To join me for dinner. I am a widower and would enjoy thy company. And perhaps I might show thee about New York? It is unusual for me to meet a woman with such a fine appreciation for the law."

Madame Knight fluttered her stubby eyelashes.

Philena smiled. "She also—"

"Writes poetry, sir," Hester added.

Mr. Cook looked impressed. For the first time in ever so long, blushing Madame Knight gave Hester and Philena appreciative glances.

The twins did not notice. They were too busy admiring their precious green and yellow keepsakes. *Someone loved us.* Hester touched the ribbons. She looked at Philena.

Philena nodded. *Someone loved us very much indeed.*

Polly winked mischievously at the two sisters. "Do you suppose when these ribbons were removed from your baby curls, my dear old grandmother may have mixed you up?"

"What do you mean?" Hester asked.

Philena understood. She grinned. "Perhaps I am really Hester." She turned to her twin. "And you —"

"Are really Philena." Hester smiled. The sound of the three girls' laughter echoed out of the room and down the grand hallway. And for the first time, Mr. Edward Cook's house was filled with the unmistakable sound of surprising, sudden joy.

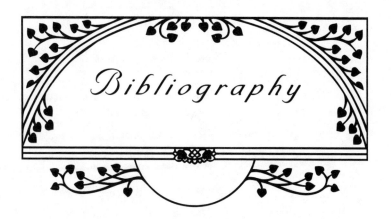

Bibliography

Botkin, B. A. *New England Folklore*. New York: Bonanza Books, 1965.

Crawford, Mary Caroline. *Social Life in Old New England*. Boston: Little, Brown and Co., 1914.

Cronon, William. *Changes in the Land: Indians, Colonists and the Ecology of New England*. New York: Hill and Wang, 1983.

Daniels, Bruce C. *Puritans at Play: Leisure and Recreation in Colonial New England*. New York: St. Martin's Griffin, 1995.

Deetz, James. *In Small Things Forgotten: The Archeology of Early American Life*. New York: Doubleday, 1977.

Dow, George Francis. *Everyday Life in the Massachusetts Bay Colony*. New York: Dover Publications, 1988.

Earle, Alice Morse. *Child Life in Colonial Days*. New York: Macmillan, 1899.

――――. *Customs and Fashions in Old New England*. New York: Charles Scribner's Sons, 1904.

Freiberg, Malcolm, editor. *The Journal of Madame Knight*. Boston: David R. Godine, 1972.

Hawke, David Freeman. *Everyday Life in Early America*. New York: Harper & Row, 1988.

Holbrook, Stewart H. *The Old Post Road*. New York: McGraw-Hill Book Co., 1962.

Marx, Jenifer. *Pirates and Privateers of the Caribbean*. Malibar, FL: Krieger Publishing Co., 1992.

Mitchell, Edwin V. *It's an Old New England Custom*. New York: Vanguard Press, Inc., 1946.

Ross, Marjorie Drake. *The Book of Boston: The Colonial Period*. New York: Hastings House Publishers, 1960.

Ulrich, Laurel Thatcher. *Good Wives: Image and Reality in the Lives of Women in Northern New England, 1650–1750*. New York: Random House, 1991.

Wolf, Stephanie Grauman. *As Various As Their Land: The Everyday Lives of Eighteenth-Century Americans*. New York: HarperCollins Publishers, 1993.

About the Author

Trained as a journalist, Laurie Lawlor worked for many years as a freelance writer and editor before devoting herself full-time to the creation of children's books. She enjoys many speaking engagements at schools and libraries, and her books have been nominated for many awards. She lives in Evanston, Illinois, with her husband, son, daughter, and two large Labrador retrievers. Her books include the *Addie Across the Prairie* series, the *Heartland* series, *How to Survive Third Grade*, *The Worm Club*, *Gold in the Hills*, and *Little Women* (a movie novelization). Her nonfiction work, *Shadow Catcher: The Life and Work of Edward S. Curtis*, won the Carl Sandburg Award for nonfiction (1995) and the Golden Kite Honor Book Award (1995).